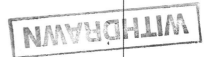

Prologue

After it was all over, I never knew who to blame: myself for thinking that I could leave my familiar life behind and remain unscathed, or myself for counting on the touring company to supply me with Life's Great Adventure. Either way, I was fully culpable.

When it was all said and done I was one unhappy camper.

I left my home in Piney Woods with the hope that I'd never be back and with the sage advice of Crazy Great-Aunt Opal ringing in my ears: 'Shut the door when you leave'. Of course, she was referring to the door of her assisted-living luxury apartment, 'built with your comfort in mind', and not the metaphorical door that swung shut behind me when I joined *Becklaw's Murder Mystery Tour* as a 'character actor'. Still, it was good advice, apropos to almost any situation.

My mother, the one-time belle of Piney Woods, Louisiana, was absolutely appalled at my decision to leave the stone monstrosity known as the Anderson Family Home. According to her, I should be focused on taming a man, bearing his children, and settling down in my own domicile. Since none of those options appealed to me, I was determined to get out as soon as possible.

From the moment that I first spotted the *Sears and Roebuck Wish Book* as a child and realized that something existed outside of our tiny burg, I was determined to see it for myself. Life, so far, had consisted of family Sundays, followed by a week of prescribed activities, ending again in the ubiquitous Sunday get-togethers. It was, in a word, boring.

Thankfully, I had siblings to distract me. Being the only girl in a family of seven brothers, I was alternately loved, harassed, petted, bossed, and protected, and I still consider the Seven Brothers Boot Camp as the single reason I was able to recover so quickly from what came to be known as the 'Jo leaves Piney Woods and Discovers a Dead Body or Two' incident.

It didn't happen quite like that, as you might guess.

Chapter One

The morning was chamber-of-commerce perfect: azure skies tinged with the remains of a spectacular sunrise, a light breeze, and moderate temperatures. I stood at my closet trying to decide what to wear. My destination was Copper, Colorado, and I'd heard rumors that it was still cold in that part of the country. I finally settled on my go-to jeans, a long-sleeved thermal under a T-shirt, and a denim jacket. High-top tennis shoes completed my ensemble, and I felt ready to face any challenge – or weather change – the day might bring.

My mother's bedroom door was closed when I passed it, and I stood for a moment trying to discern any sounds. Hearing none, I blew a kiss in the general direction of where she might have been standing had she come out to see me off and reached the front door just as the taxi's horn blared.

Merla Mae Bonner Anderson, my mother and current matriarch of the Anderson clan, had definite ideas of how a young woman should behave, and leaving home to join a traveling acting troupe was not on the top of her list. I tried to explain it to her, showing her the brochure that had caught my fancy and had given me the impetus to get out of Dodge, so to speak. My seven brothers were jealous, happy, indifferent, and supportive, depending on whom I was speaking to at any given moment. My best friend

Neva Anderson (no relation, as far as we know) was excited for me, but content to stay put.

'You can send me postcards, Jo,' she had said, stroking Merlin, the moth-eaten excuse for a cat that she doted on. It, of course, said nothing, instead wrinkling its pug-like nose at me. That could be construed as a comment, I suppose.

It was through Neva's odd occupation that I was now a full-fledged member of Becklaw's Murder Mystery Tour, or at least that's how I remembered it. She was a prolific subscriber to magazines of all sorts, from *TV Guide* to *Soap Opera Digest* to *National Geographic*, and in the back of one of them she spotted an advertisement asking for character actors. I filled out the application, jumped through some logistical hoops, and almost overnight became part of a traveling troupe based in Copper, Colorado.

My mother had retired early the evening before, claiming a migraine, but we all knew she was just miffed at my decision to leave. The family had gathered to say farewell and wish me luck, and I guess I was expecting something like that from her. Which is why I had to kiss the air goodbye, instead of her soft, scented cheek. I was being punished.

Train service is sporadic at best in our neck of the country, so imagine my surprise when the 07:32 to Denver arrived at 07:32. Tossing away my lukewarm cup of station coffee, I grabbed up the two bags I had packed the night before and leapt up the steps into the passenger car. I chose a seat at the very back, hoping to snooze a bit on the eight hour trip. Since that was my plan, of course it didn't happen that way. For some reason, I tend to attract either chatty older women, alarmingly like Crazy Great-Aunt Opal, or harried young mothers with at least three crabby, fidgety children. For this train trip, I got both.

Two very sick children, one convoluted conversation (this with a dotty old woman whose lavender hair kept toppling down her forehead), and eight very long hours later, my train arrived at the Denver railway station. We who were disembarking stood up, stretched our atrophied limbs, and climbed stiffly down the steel steps. I joined the horde of bodies moving toward the covered depot, scanning the throng for someone holding a sign reading 'Becklaw's'.

I quickly spotted a short, plump woman standing off to one side of the platform, her truncated arms attempting to hold the sign up high enough to be read above the multitude. Making my way over to her, I sat down my bags, stuck out my hand, and introduced myself.

'I'm Josephine Anderson, ma'am, here for Becklaw's,' I stated as proudly as if I had announced my arrival in the White House. 'I usually go by "Jo".'

She lowered the sign, groaning a little as her arms came down from their perch above her gray head. 'I'm Beatrice Becklaw, owner, proprietor, whatever. Glad you made it safely, Jo. And call me Miss Bea.'

I stared at her, somewhat shocked at her proclamation. For some reason, I had created a Mr Becklaw in my mind, a man whose presence would be both noble and noticeable. The person who stood in front of me was certainly neither. Without attempting to curb my staring, I looked her over: she was short, as I had already noticed, solidly built with plenty of cushion around the middle, and had a head full of untamed frizz that was scraped back as flat as she could get it to go. The part that wasn't held down by a series of combs and pins stuck up in tiny patches, much like a bed of sea anemone waving in the ocean current. Still, her face was kind, and I could see that she would be a no-nonsense, commonsensical type of boss.

We shook hands, her grasp surprisingly firm. 'There should be three more folks joining us, so we'll hang out here for a little while, if you don't mind.' Miss Bea turned away from me, standing on tiptoe as she surveyed the people milling about the station.

I noticed a very tall young man standing to one side, a look of bewilderment on his large face. Next to him stood a young woman who seemed more concerned with applying lipstick than finding whomever it was she was there to meet.

'Ah. I think I've spotted two. Jo, you go over there and grab them. It'll be that huge man and the girl with him. I'll keep an eye out for the other. Go on now,' she ordered, all but clapping her hands at me.

I scooted, leaving my bags at her feet and hoping that no one would take them. The pair watched my approach, he with trepidation and she with bored detachment.

'I'm here from Becklaw's. Are you two ...?' My question hung incomplete in the air between us.

'Yep. That would be us. I'm Leslie Newsome. This is Little John Smythe.'

Was she kidding?

Little John – if that was really his name – leaned down and effortlessly gathered up the myriad bags nestled by their feet. They followed me back to where Miss Bea stood, this time with slender young man at her side.

'Miss Beatrice Becklaw, this is Leslie Newsome and Little John Smythe. Leslie, Little John, this is Miss Bea.' I felt absolutely foolish uttering this introduction and I noticed that the other man made no attempt to hide his amused smile.

'I'm Derek Robertson.' He held out his hand and I noticed that, for all his slight appearance, his handshake was strong. I think that Little John noticed it as well because the look in his timid eyes got even more pronounced. I grinned to myself. This was going to be fun. We all turned to face Miss Bea, waiting for a directive.

'We're all here now, so we'd best be getting on to the lodge. You boys carry the bags. Jo, take this sign and put it in the trash bin. Leslie, you come help me down the stairs. Everyone ready?' She looked around, her eyes as bright as a young girl's. I could tell that she was definitely in her element.

We trooped *en masse* down the platform steps and onto the sidewalk that ran straight out to the parking lot. Near the edge of the lot I spied an old panel-sided station wagon, reminiscent of the vehicles my mother would drive in my childhood. That would be a Miss Bea-type of transportation, I thought.

I was right.

We piled into the wagon, Miss Bea taking the driver's seat. She sat, I noticed, suspiciously higher than she should have, considering her stature. Taking a quick peek over the front seat, I spotted the pillow on which she had plumped her rather generous backside. I met Derek's eyes in the rearview mirror and we grinned at each other. We were thinking the same thing, I was sure.

The drive out of the town and into the area outside of Denver was absolutely breathtaking. Having never been further from home than Alexandria, which was built squarely on a series of flat areas that fed into swampland, I was amazed at the size of the mountains surrounding me. The tops were still capped in white magnificence, the snow too high up to melt. The road, although a modern thoroughfare of divided highway, felt more like a magic carpet taking me further and further away from reality.

And I was more than ready.

The lodge – it was really an old house with a verandah snaking around all sides – was set back from the main road by way of a dirt path. I caught glimpses of the house as we bumped up the trail, passing trees glorious with new green leaves and fields of what appeared to be daisies. I must have sighed aloud in my delight, because Miss Bea chuckled.

'I completely agree with you, Jo. It *is* lovely, isn't it?' She twirled the steering wheel in her dimpled hands and suddenly we were there, rolling to a stop in front of the house that was to be our base for the next six months.

I carried my bags up the steps of the house and into the screened porch. An odd assortment of chairs and tables stood about as if flung there by accident, and a series of doors marched down the length of the front wall that presented itself to us.

Miss Bea, struggling up the stairs with help from Derek, pointed with her chin at the door in the middle of the wall. 'Jo, open that door, please. It shouldn't be locked.'

I obeyed, a reflex honed by years of living with my mother and brothers. The door creaked a bit as I turned the knob, an old affair constructed of brass that had tarnished with time. The inside of the house was dim and cool, and I heard a faint scuttling sound somewhere to the right. I jumped.

'It's only a mouse, Jo,' said Miss Bea briskly. 'Nothing that can hurt you. Boys, you take the rooms at the very top of the stairs. Girls, you'll have the rooms on the second floor. I use the bedroom down here. Hustle now. I want to have a quick meeting in the front parlor just as soon as you get your rooms settled.'

We hustled.

Leslie and I moved up the short hallway that led from

the landing. Three closed doors lined the hall, and we opened all of them, peering in cautiously. I'm not sure of what I expected, considering the apparent age of the house, but what we found was comforting.

Two of the rooms had a large bed smack-dab in the middle of the room, a tall chest of drawers, a small table that functioned as a nightstand, and a rocking chair that sat in the far corner. There was the scent of newness in the air, and it occurred to me that the comforters and sheets were brand new. I took the room nearest the stairs, and Leslie the one next to that.

The third door opened up to a modern bathroom, complete with towel warmer and glassed-in shower. I briefly wondered if the rest of the house would prove as well-heeled. Miss Bea, in spite of her second-hand aura, must have money.

I could hear the sounds of footsteps tromping above me as I moved back into the hall and down the stairs toward the parlor as directed. The loud thumps would be Little John and the quicker footsteps would be those of Derek, I surmised. I already liked him. As for Little John, I would reserve judgment.

In a few short minutes we were all gathered together, seated on the various chairs and sofas placed throughout the rather large and airy room. Tall windows added to the feeling of spaciousness, and I was glad that there were no draperies to hide the fantastic view.

Miss Bea stood in the center of the parlor, hands clasped in front of her and lips pursed as if in thought. I suppose she *was* thinking, since she looked at each of us in turn, turning slowly, not speaking. She cleared her throat.

'Folks, I am delighted to welcome you to Becklaw's Murder Mystery Tour. It is my hope we can all work together to entertain the vast audiences that may call upon our skills, and that we will enjoy each other's company.

You will each have a specific character to portray, but we'll get into that tomorrow. For the rest of today, I want you to talk to each other, explore the house and the grounds, and get some good rest. We leave in four days for our first engagement. Dinner will be ready promptly at six o'clock.'

She looked around the room again, those bright eyes missing nothing as she scanned our faces. I noticed that she looked a bit tired, but if she had settled this entire house by herself, I would expect her to feel that way.

With a sweet smile for all of us, Miss Bea left the room. I looked at Leslie, wondering if there would be a camaraderie based on our shared femaleness. She was staring at Derek with a frank expression of something akin to speculation on her face, and Little John sat looking at his large paw of a hand, picking at his fingernails and not meeting anyone's eyes.

Since I had arrived first, I felt something of a responsibility for getting everyone over this first awkward silence. I cleared my throat, much as Miss Bea had done, and turned to Derek.

'Have you had much experience with character acting?' The words sounded stilted, and I could feel the beginnings of a blush working its way up from my neck to my face.

Thankfully, he chose to rescue me from my own discomfort. 'Actually, this is my first time acting at anything. You?' His eyebrows lifted a tad in query as he looked back at me.

'It's my first attempt at acting as well. That's weird that she'd hire two newbie actors at one time, don't you think?'

Leslie shifted in her seat, reaching over to pat Little John's massive thigh. 'It's our first try as well. Do you think that Miss Bea is a little, well, off her rocker or something?'

Frankly, I was stumped. I had no idea how anyone, Miss Bea included, would be able to whip us into fighting form within four short days.

We were soon to find out.

Chapter Two

Dinner was a quiet affair, but that was largely due to the fact that we were fully occupied with consuming the meal Miss Bea had set before us. And what a meal it was! Thickly sliced, broiled pork chops smothered in mushrooms and topped with pan gravy, tender baby carrots and peas swimming in a garlic sauce, a salad that would delight the staunchest vegetarian, and steaming rolls that oozed honey butter. I decided right then and there that if I did nothing else but eat this way for the next six months, the entire adventure would be worth it. When Miss Bea disappeared into the kitchen and returned carrying a huge apple pie, I couldn't help myself. I groaned aloud in pure bliss.

We four newcomers managed a desultory conversation over dessert. Mugs of coffee materialized in front of us, and between this restorative and the general feeling of camaraderie that had settled over the group, I think we managed to create the beginnings of the bond that would eventually hold as firmly as the tightest-knit family.

This turned out to be a lifesaver for me, both literally and figuratively, and I sensed that from that dinner forward, the four of us, led by the bundle of energy that was Miss Beatrice Becklaw, would be able to do whatever it was she required of us.

I finally made my drowsy way up to bed, Leslie not far

behind. From the racket I could hear coming from the top floor, I assumed 'the boys', as Miss Bea referred to them, were doing something similar.

I must have fallen into a deep sleep the moment my head hit the pillow. I had dreaded this first night somewhat, unsure of my ability to dispel homesickness in spite of my insistence on leaving my aforementioned home.

Apparently I would be fine.

When I awoke the next morning, it was to the clamor of birds perched in the branches of the ash tree just outside my window. I suppose I had always heard the birds that populated the trees in my town, but these particular creatures seemed set on waking up the entire state of Colorado. At any rate, I was wide awake and ready to get the day started.

Tossing the duvet back – it was down-filled and absolutely delicious to snuggle under – I slipped out of bed in my usual fashion, feet feeling around the floor for the slippers I had put there the night before. I must have reacted instinctively to the wriggling that my toes encountered, because I suddenly found myself standing at the bedside, the offending slippers slung clear across the room.

Leslie came barging in, her eyes as wide as mine felt.

'What in the world, Jo?'

'I – the mouse – it was in ...' I couldn't string a coherent sentence together, but I'm pretty sure that she got the gist because she leapt straight onto the middle of my bed, feet tucked under the voluminous nightgown she wore.

I cautiously crept across the room toward the offending slippers and crouched down, picking up the nearest one with my fingertips. Instantly I dropped it, leaping straight into the air as if trying to launch myself skyward and away from the scared little creature that was scampering in circles around my bare feet. Apparently this had become funny in the time it took for Leslie to see that she wasn't in the path of the vicious rodent (at least it looked vicious to me), because she burst out laughing.

'Oh, my word! You look so comical, Jo!'

I glared over my shoulder at her, failing to find the hilarity in my mousey situation.

By this time, the boys (I had begun thinking of them this way as well) had come galloping down the stairs, and I sent up a silent prayer that they had remembered to cover themselves before arriving to save the damsels in distress. My plea was heard, thankfully, and Derek and Little John, in bathrobes and slippers, burst into my room, stopping short when they saw Leslie rolling around on my bed in uncontrolled mirth and me glowering in the corner holding a slipper in my hand.

Derek was going to be the tactful member of the bunch, I could see. He looked from Leslie to me, walked over and took the slipper from my hand, then led me over to the rocking chair. Without comment, he bent down, scooped the trembling mouse into tender hands, and walked out the room, Little John trailing behind him. All done in silence. No recriminations, no sarcastic observations, no amused smiles.

He could give my brothers a lesson or two on how to treat a lady.

Somehow I managed to retrieve the dignity that had gone to tatters during my 'mouse dance', as Leslie referred to it when we spoke about it much, much later. I walked to the bathroom, took a shower, and dressed for the day, all without incident. At the breakfast table, Little John was careful to drop his eyes whenever I looked in his direction, and Derek's carefully composed face caused Miss Bea to lift quizzical eyebrows in my direction. I wasn't saying anything, though.

As far as I was concerned, the incident was closed.

I assisted Miss Bea in clearing the table, and Leslie and Little John did KP duty. Derek retrieved the paper that had appeared on the front porch, although how a paper boy (paper person?) managed to get one out this far was a mystery. With the morning chores completed, we all settled back into the front parlor that would be our main gathering spot for the duration of the week.

Miss Bea plumped herself down, the newspaper on her almost non-existent lap, a mug of coffee nearby. She looked, for all money, like a woman without a care in the world, and I knew that couldn't possibly be true, not with the four of us to coach into some semblance of acting. But I wasn't going to interrupt what was probably her regular morning routine, and no one else spoke up either.

Finally, she folded the paper carefully, set it down on the floor beside her chair, and folded her dimpled hands in her lap.

'So,' she began, her eyes traveling around the room, looking at each of us in turn, 'today will be your first day as an actor. I chose you four specifically because you had no previous acting experience, and I have every confidence that you can pull this off.'

Here, Miss Bea stopped speaking and smiled at some point above our heads. I was tempted to turn around and see what – or who – she was looking at.

'First things first,' she began briskly, her mind and eyes returning to the task at hand. Quickly she began laying out the plan she had concocted for the Becklaw's Murder Mystery Tour.

'I want to present a mystery to the audience that is easy enough to follow and hard enough that it takes some time to solve. Jo, you will be the saloon owner in our Western-themed show. Derek, you will play the bartender and the bouncer,' – here Little John looked over at Derek with something like amazement on his broad face – 'and, Leslie, you will be the drinks girl and dancer. Any questions, comments so far? Good. Little John, you will be the piano player and help Derek keep order. Wherever we play, I'll hire a few bit-part actors to fill in the story line.'

Miss Bea stood and walked across the room to a large armoire. Tugging the doors open, she reached inside and began disgorging the contents, tossing feather boas, bowler hats, leather chaps, and all manner of Western wear – or what I assumed to be Western wear – on the living room floor.

Catching up a short lilac-colored dress with lace flounces running down the sides, she tossed it over to Leslie, who caught it neatly in manicured hands. It had a train that fell from the waist and ended just above the floor, and I could envision Leslie in a get-up like that. Derek got the bowler and a striped vest, a bow tie and a collarless white shirt; I was handed a rather staid frock, at least in comparison to Leslie's lacy number, complete with high-buttoned shoes. I was amazed at the manner in which Miss Bea had gauged our sizes and shapes, simply from the application in the magazine. Little John, it appeared, presented a bit more of a challenge.

With Little John finally squared away, we all trooped upstairs to our respective rooms to change into our costumes and, hopefully, into our new characters. I had suggested that we each use our true names as that would eliminate the need to remember who we were on any given day, and Miss Bea readily agreed. So within the space of a few minutes, I transformed from Jo Anderson, newly arrived from Piney Woods and a clannish existence, to Jo Anderson, owner and proprietress of a Western saloon. It was heady stuff indeed.

We reassembled in the living room. Leslie looked spectacular in the dancer's outfit, and I could see that Derek and Little John thoroughly agreed with me. Derek's barman costume added an air of decorum to his slight size, and I noticed Leslie's sidelong glances aimed in his direction. Little John, clad in a pair of corduroy trousers and a tunic-like shirt, sat shyly on his chair, sending bashful looks at Leslie. I, in my no-nonsense black school marm's dress and high-heeled boots, surveyed the others and grinned. We looked nothing if not authentic. Miss Bea had done her homework.

The rest of the day was spent in learning how to speak 'Western'. Miss Bea taught us the slang, the accent, and the tone that she had envisioned for us. I, being from Louisiana and therefore already blessed with what Miss Bea called a 'real Southern drawl', fared the best at the tutelage. The others struggled with this a bit more, but by the end of that first full day, we were more than character actors: We *were* the characters.

I could see that Miss Bea was very proud of us all.

I cooked dinner that evening, with assistance from Leslie and Derek. It was a simple dish, one of my favorites and usually a big hit with my picky brothers. Chicken breasts were pounded a bit, to thin them out, and then layered in a baking dish with prosciutto, mushrooms, and mozzarella. As it baked, I set about creating my favorite pasta side dish: penne with pesto sauce and roasted red bell peppers. A simple green salad completed the meal, and within a short while we were at the dining room table eating and chatting as if we had known each other all of our lives. I suppose in a way that was true: we had created new lives for ourselves and we were all in on it from the beginning.

Not willing to have a repeat performance of the mouse incident, I had set a few 'green traps' around my room and had secured my slippers under my pillow. I shuddered. If a mouse managed to get to them while I slept, I would come unglued. Hopefully, the relatives of the mouse that had started all of the commotion had been notified of my intentions and would remain far, far away.

Or sleep in Derek's room. He didn't seem to mind the little critters in the least.

Chapter Three

The next few days flew by as we ate, slept, and spoke inside our characters' skins. I was called 'Miss Jo' by the cast, and even Miss Bea began to refer to me by that handle. Little John became 'LJ', a much easier sobriquet, I thought, though Derek and Leslie retained their own names. I suppose it was due to my character's position as saloon owner that moved me to the front of the pack, and it soon became clear to me that everyone had started relying on my opinions and guidance in our quest for authenticity. That was quite amusing, especially since I was no more a Western saloon owner than they were barman, dancer, and piano player. Well, LJ really *did* play the piano, and beautifully, too. He alone could perform his role with some air of assurance that he knew what he was doing.

The worst part about my character was her choice of footwear. The high-heeled boots, resplendent with shiny black buttons marching down the front of each, were nice to look at but pure torture to wear on a daily basis. That, combined with the myriad layers of petticoats and waist-cinching girdle under my dress, made me fervently grateful for modern clothing styles. Still, if Miss Jo, saloon owner and proprietress, wore this garb, I would as well. I would suffer for my craft.

Friday night materialized more quickly than I had

anticipated. After three solid days of being in character, Derek, LJ, Leslie, and I were ready to begin acting. It still amazed me, though, how soon our first gig had arrived.

We were the featured event at the Copper Moose Lodge Annual Barbecue and Chili Dinner. I guess the menu inspired them to ask us, or maybe it was the fact that John Hamilton, lodge leader and Western buff, was also a good friend of Miss Bea's. Either way it was fine by me. I was rarin' to get goin' (see how casually I slipped into Western lingo?).

The Lodge was some five miles away, reachable by a two-lane road that led into town. I was thankful Miss Bea hadn't taken the highway; the day had been a drizzly one and I was sure the surface would be slick from oil. Although I knew Miss Bea would be careful, I didn't trust the other drivers I had observed in the few short days I had been here. Either they didn't notice the sheer drops into rock-strewn canyons any more, or they had a death wish. Whatever the reason, I was glad not to be on the road with them tonight.

The lights of the Moose Lodge blazed out across the gravel parking lot, emphasizing the many pot holes and wheel-rutted parking slots. Miss Bea slipped the wagon into one marked 'Reserved for Guest' and cut the motor. We were all silent for once, and I think that stage fright had made its first ugly appearance. The crickets were in fine voice following the showers, but I swear I could hear my heart thudding above their chirping. It was probably just the thumping rhythm of the music emanating from the open door, though.

The Lodge was packed and dinner already in full swing. Five rather nervous-looking young people stood huddled by the entrance, and Miss Bea gave them a cheerful wave.

'There're your bit-parters,' she announced, indicating

the quintet with a nod of her frizzled head.

I know that I have mentioned the condition of Miss Bea's hair before, and tonight it was in full frizz, thanks to the dampness in the night air. She had carefully smoothed it back from her forehead, placing pins and combs in random spots to hold it down. Still, it managed to have a life of its own, and the end result was a coiffure that defied gravity. And hairspray.

I think I admired her more for what I saw as her only deficiency.

We managed to get inside without too much hoopla and back to the dressing rooms behind the red velvet curtain that hung near the front of the room. The five temps followed us warily. I think they thought that Miss Bea was going to personally strip them down and dress them in saloon-appropriate regalia.

Three of them were to play cardsharps; carrying on, drinking (root beer) and a playing a high-stakes poker game. They joined LJ and Derek in the room marked 'Men's' and soon appeared duded out in cowboy boots, jeans, and leather vests. The other two actors were young women, set to play another dancer and a 'lady of the night', respectively. Their clothes were a bit harder to judge, but Miss Bea had once again pulled a miracle out of her traveling garment bag. Lydia, a shy girl and daughter of John Hamilton was dressed in a lacy number much like Leslie's, and I saw with amusement that she kept trying to tug it down in the back. This in turn caused the neckline to plunge even further, and the poor girl was scarlet with effort and embarrassment. Miss Bea didn't seem to notice her discomfort, so I didn't either.

Lyssa, Lydia's younger sister and apparently born with a much worldlier attitude, reveled in her costume as a 'loose woman'. She was also tugging at her dress, but she intended for the neckline to drop just as far as it could possibly go. When she stuck her head out of the curtain to look at the crowd, her mother must have seen more than she wanted to. Mrs Hamilton joined us, mouth prim and a safety pin in her hands. She went to work on Lyssa's dress and fixed that girl's exhibitionist streak but good. I shook my head. I am always amazed at how different siblings can be.

Miss Bea gathered us around her for one last pep talk. I noticed that LJ's forehead was beaded in sweat, tiny pearls of moisture that stayed miraculously in place.

Leslie looked almost bored she was so calm, and Derek looked stern. I couldn't see my own face, of course, but I felt the tell-tale flush that creeps into place whenever I am nervous. I sincerely hoped that it looked becoming and not blotchy.

'Derek, you'll stay behind the bar for most of the hour, only coming out to wipe down tables,' began Miss Bea. 'LJ, the piano is set up at stage left, and you need to go right over to it as soon as the curtain opens. Start playing something like "Oh, Susannah". Leslie, you and Lydia will circulate among the tables on stage as well as those in the audience. Chat, laugh, refresh their drinks, whatever. Lyssa, you won't come out until you hear LJ begin playing "The Girl He Left Behind". Your job is just to strut around and give all the men some steamy looks.' Here Lyssa looked ecstatic and Lydia looked alarmed.

'Miss Jo, you'll be walking around all over the place, making sure that everyone is comfy. You three boys,' – here she indicated the cowboys, who elbowed each other and grinned – 'will be at the center table playing a game of poker. Make a big deal of talking and drinking and all that. Shuffle the cards as fancy as you can. When Miss Jo walks over to your table, start showing off, and one of you will get mad and stomp off.

'That's your cue, Lyssa, to run after him. Once you're off-stage, you'll scream then run back on, yelling that he's crazy. You'll then exit at the opposite side of the stage, saying that you're going upstairs to rest up for the night. After a few minutes, he'll come back onstage and go up to the bar then leave again and the other two will follow you out, jeering and picking a fight.

'Leslie will make an excuse to run upstairs to talk to Lyssa, then come down screaming that she's been murdered. Got it?'

She consulted her copious notes, making sure that nothing had been left out.

'And don't stress, folks. This is about as casual as it gets.'

'Miss Bea?' One of the cowboy trio raised his hand as if he was in school. 'Who is the killer?'

Miss Bea stared at him as if he had sprouted horns and a tail, then burst out laughing. 'I clean forgot that part! Quick, someone – who should it be?'

'I could do it,' offered LJ quietly. I looked at him with my mouth wide open. I had no idea he had it in him.

'OK. This is what we'll do: when the three *amigos* leave, you stand up from the piano and say something about needing a break. You then tell Miss Jo that you have to run upstairs for a moment. You stay gone for about two minutes. After that, Leslie will go upstairs and 'discover' the body. I think that after Lyssa screams about you being crazy,' – she jabbed her forefinger into the leather-clad chest of the first cowboy – 'most people will have you pegged as the murderer. If not, and it's too easy, we'll change it up for our next gig. OK, if that's all, let's get a move on.'

Dear reader, I had an absolute blast that first performance, miscues and all. I was transformed totally into Miss Jo, saloon owner and peacekeeper. The audience was appreciative of our efforts, although I suspect that they 'solved' the murder very quickly. The local talent took many curtain calls, bowing to uproarious applause.

Miss Bea got the biggest recognition of all, as well she should. Her beaming face and waving hair included everyone in her smile. I was so happy for her, this woman whose dream was to direct a great masterpiece of the stage.

If this was what it was like to be an actress, I was hooked.

The ride back to our house was punctuated with laughter and joking comments directed at the way that Derek twirled his towel and Leslie teetered around the stage on high heels. LJ's face blushed when I mentioned his choice of entrance song, "Happy Birthday to You". I laughed outright when Derek reminded me of my Louisiana accent that had crept unawares back into my speech.

'You sounded like "Daisy Mae Meets the Wild West",' he hooted, and I had to agree. I would have to work harder on my Western dialogue.

Miss Bea drove silently, a quiet smile tucked into the corners of her mouth. She was tired, but we all were. I mentally predicted a quick bedtime and a long snooze for one and all.

I was wrong.

It was sometime after one in the morning that I was awakened by a dull thump and the sound of something rolling across the floor below. I lay completely still, listening as hard as I could. Had the field mice joined forces and invaded? I sincerely hoped not. One mouse was one too many as far as I was concerned.

No one else seemed to have heard it. I could detect no sounds of footsteps or doors opening, so I cautiously leaned across to the lamp that sat on my bedside and pulled the little chain that hung down from its bulb. The click of the light coming on seemed extra loud, so I waited, frozen, straining to hear noises from downstairs.

A discomforting thought flashed into my mind: why hadn't Miss Bea heard it? Or was it she that I was hearing? Or – I crossed my fingers – only someone up and getting a drink of water from the kitchen?

Or, heaven forbid, it was an intruder.

I made up my mind. Swinging my legs off the bed and fishing under my pillow for my slippers, I opened my bedroom door as softly as possible. Pausing on the landing, I began to tiptoe down the stairs, sending up a silent prayer that I would miss the squeaky step that was second from the bottom. Or was it the third?

It was the third.

The wooden shriek that it emitted when I put my full weight on it was loud enough to wake the dead. I could hear doors popping open all over the house, and the sound of the screen door on the front porch slamming closed as someone in their haste to leave banged hard into it.

Miss Bea stumbled out of her room, her head full of those pink cushiony rollers that my mother used to put into my hair to coax it into curls. Her eyes were bleary, and I could see right away that she had no idea what had happened.

Derek came thumping down the stairs, a little unsteady in his slippered feet. His face was full of concern, and he looked ready to do battle with whatever forces of evil might be lurking about.

'What's going on?' he demanded, hands on his slight

hips and a frown creasing his brow.

Miss Bea turned to me, as did the rest of the troupe who now stood huddled together.

'I have no earthly idea,' I admitted. 'Something woke me up, I came to see what it was, and then someone ran out of the front door.' I looked from one face to the other.

Derek spun on his heels, no mean feat in slippers, and marched to the front door. Without touching it, he used one foot to pull the slightly ajar door more fully open, then leaned out and scanned the verandah.

'No one's out there that I can see,' he reported, then pulled his head back in the door. 'Miss Jo, did you actually see anyone down here?'

That flush I mentioned before, the one that gets blotchy sometimes? It appeared almost instantly, and I could tell by the alarmed look in Derek's eyes that I looked a bit, well, unbalanced.

'Hold on there, girl,' he admonished, hands raised before him in a placating gesture. 'I don't mean that you imagined it, but ...' His words trailed off, not really apologizing but not admitting he was wrong, either.

Nice. Between mouse issues and phantom noises in the night, I was rapidly becoming the troupe weirdo.

Chapter Four

Somehow we all got back to our assorted rooms without a brawl breaking out. No one was thrilled about being awakened in the middle of the night for what might be a figment of my wild imagination. Leslie muttered and threw dark looks at me as we climbed the stairs, and even LJ showed his disapproval by stomping a bit more loudly than usual. Derek, as per usual, reserved comment.

Apparently no one remembered the open front door.

Breakfast was subdued, not much in the way of conversation but with a lot of eye rubbing and yawning. It was safe to surmise that this was the worst night since our arrival in Copper. Even Miss Bea, normally chipper and ready to rock no matter the time of day, seemed a bit under the weather. Her hair, normally just frizzy, was both curly and frizzy this morning. Her head looked like a Brillo pad had landed there and exploded, corkscrew curls fighting for autonomy amidst the requisite pins.

I decided that someone needed to say something, and since I was Miss Jo, leader of the band, I voted on myself. It went a little like this:

'So, has anyone bothered to check outside for the paper this morning? Or look for footprints of whoever was in our house in the middle of the night?'

The response sounded like this:

... Well, actually there was no sound to accompany the three glares from my fellow actors or the look of pity from Miss Bea. So, having been brought up in a house where you never say "never", I tried again. This time I roused the troops and got an earful.

Leslie went first, apparently since she was the one who shared the bathroom with me and therefore felt entitled to first dibs in telling me off.

'Jo, I have no idea what you heard, or thought that you heard, only ...' – here a glance at the clock on the sideboard – '... five and one-half hours ago, but I can tell you that I heard nothing, saw nothing, and regret not having a full night's sleep.' Her glowering face told me that I might come to regret this as well.

Next in line was Derek, his normally calm features rearranged into a look akin to disdain.

'I'm positive the door was open when we went to sleep last night, Jo. I can't imagine anyone actually coming here and breaking in. And even if it wasn't already open, no one ever comes around here anyway.'

He looked so smug that I felt compelled to point out that the paper person managed to come around every morning. This earned me a derisive snort from Leslie.

LJ, bless his reticent heart, took a 'pass' in the game of "Kick Jo When She's Down". I gave him the benefit of my sunniest smile, which sent a ripple of color across his face. This earned me another glare from Leslie.

Finally, it was Miss Bea's turn.

To my surprise, and also to my delight, Miss Bea took my side. If I hadn't already begun to admire the woman, this would have been the start.

'I happen to find your tale quite believable, my dear.' I

smiled in triumph at the others, relishing their looks of incredulity.

She continued in a matter-of-fact tone, 'I think that you might have encountered a local scourge known as raccoons.' This sounded so ridiculous that I burst out laughing, causing Leslie to give me the 'stare of death' with eyes narrowed to virtual slits in her face.

That girl needed to be careful; her face could freeze like that one day and then where would her acting career be?

The idea that forest creatures could actually manipulate doors and find their way into a house without the aid of a human repelled me. Never one to glory in animated movies featuring sweet fawns bounding playfully through trees or birds chirping merrily as they did housework, I felt a smidgeon of fear tiptoe from the recess of my mind and go tripping down my spine. Visions of mice and raccoons in cahoots, planning feverishly to run me out of town, gave me a sudden headache.

This called for serious strategizing. This was war.

Despite Miss Bea's many assurances that raccoons could not purposely hunt me down and hurt me, especially if I locked my bedroom door, I could not shake the image of a stealthily creeping animal, moving up the stairs and straight to my bedroom door in the dead of night. Leslie must have had similar thoughts. I saw her shiver and move closer to LJ, who, in turn, edged his huge body nearer to her. As upset as I was, I had to grin at the sight. Just who was comforting whom?

The troupe was feeling a bit awkward with me since Miss Bea had exonerated me of my sin. I, on the other hand, was feeling quite magnanimous, and proved it by offering to do the dishes alone.

I had hardly begun to run the water when Leslie joined me, standing off to the side as if we had never met before.

I tossed her a towel, keeping up a stream of chatter about this and that. We were soon joined by LJ, then Derek, each of the boys looking a little sheepish.

I let them all suffer for a few minutes more, then turned and gave them all a brilliant smile. 'I hope,' I said, 'that this ends the issue.'

Talking over one another, they each assured me that yes, indeed, this proved beyond the shadow of a doubt that I was both sane and sage, and did I have any plan in mind to prevent this from happening again?

Miss Jo was back in the saddle again.

I rallied the troops once again (pardon the mixing of analogies) and laid out the plans for the day. Tomorrow morning we would be picking up camp and moving to Manchester, a mountain town not too far from Copper, north-east up Highway 25 and the site for the county fair. We were booked to perform nightly at the barbecue tent, and Miss Bea wanted to meet up with the local talent a little earlier than we had for the Moose Lodge performance.

Leslie was put in charge of gathering and packing the costumes and accessories we would use. To Derek, I assigned the task of checking on our accommodation, which would be in a KOA – Kampgrounds of America – campground just outside of Manchester. I told him to make sure – doubly sure –that there would be electrical outlets. I needed my blow dryer. LJ was set to washing the faithful station wagon, shining up the tires, and vacuuming out the interior, which I felt had not been done for at least ten years. Or more.

Miss Bea kept herself occupied bustling around the house, checking that the paper delivery would be stopped for the six days we would be gone, and that someone would be coming out to fix the rather large tear in the verandah's screen door. I had to smile whenever I saw the hole left behind by the fleeing raccoon. I felt vindicated and a lot less worried about turning into a version of Crazy Great-Aunt Opal.

Just a bit of background on my family: we tend to assign names to one another, such as Crazy Great-Aunt Opal or Sleepy Uncle Pete. While there are times these names are a good indication of the type of person they are, more often than not it's a misnomer. For instance, Sleepy Uncle Pete wasn't.

That wasn't the case of Crazy Great-Aunt Opal, though. She really was a one hundred per cent, *bona fide* nutter. Some said it was because of a broken heart, others pointed to the time that she fell out of the persimmon tree and did a number on the back of her head. I personally think it's genetic, since her mother was also a bit gaga, shall we say. Which is why I was worried about myself and the "Raccoon Incident". Having Miss Bea explain what had happened gave me hope that my marbles were still together.

But I digress. As I was saying before I felt the need to explain my family's foibles, I kicked it into high gear and got the four of us moving. While LJ tended to get more water on himself than the car, he still did a passable job. At least the road salt from the winter had been removed, and the scuff marks on the tires, from where Miss Bea would often scrape the sidewalk, were gone, replaced by a high glossy shine thanks to some elbow grease and tire cleaner.

When we regrouped for a quick lunch of grilled cheese and tomato sandwiches and a heaped platter of Miss Bea's garlic home fries, Derek was able to report that our reservations for two large trailers had been confirmed, and that yes, indeed, there were both hot showers and electrical outlets in the campground's facilities.

And indoor toilets.

Leslie brought up the fact that we needed more sizes available for the dancer and 'lady of the night' costumes because, as she delicately phrased it, some would be able to 'hold up the front' and some wouldn't. Derek understood and smiled, but I could tell from the look on LJ's face that this was a concept that he didn't quite get. He was really very sweet, I had discovered, and probably needed Leslie more than she needed him. Oh, well. To each his own, I sighed inwardly.

I had spent the morning going over our roles and the plot of the performance. We had discovered several gaps in logic at the Moose Lodge dinner which, thankfully, the audience either hadn't noticed or hadn't cared about. I was determined, though, to put together a top-of-the-line murder mystery that would challenge our viewers for more than ten minutes.

By the late afternoon we had done all we could do to get ready for our first real tour. The costumes had been sorted and packed, and the boys loaded the various boxes and bags into the back of the station wagon to save time in the morning. We had each packed a suitcase of personal items, as well as a few 'modern clothes' for whenever we might have a few hours to ourselves. I didn't know about the rest of the bunch but I thoroughly intended to avail myself of the fun – and food – the county fair might have to offer.

Derek took his turn cooking that night. I suppose I expected the typical bachelor fare: pizza, hot dogs topped with canned chili beans, and the like. Much to my surprise, he served up a meal that was on par with some of the best restaurants around.

Dinner began with bowls of creamy tomato bisque, topped with a dollop of sour cream and home-made croutons. Luscious! Baskets of rolls that oozed cheddar cheese sat on the table, and I could have happily made a meal of that and the soup. The main course, though, almost blew my gastronomical expectations clear out of the water.

From the covered baking dish that Derek carried from the kitchen emanated the most tantalizing odors, and I discovered that I still had quite the appetite. Carefully placing the dish on the pizza stone that served as a table protector, Derek lifted the lid, stepping back a bit to let us savor the rosemary-scented steam.

'It's my version of raspberry-glazed chicken breasts,' he announced. I could see that he was struggling to keep the pride off of his face. Heck, if I could cook like that, I wouldn't care if I looked a bit full of myself!

'Derek, that looks absolutely divine. May I ask what's in it?' Miss Bea held out her plate for the first portion, and we all waited to hear what he had to say.

'Well, it's simply chicken breasts, boneless and skinless, of course, rubbed with rosemary, oregano, and sage then baked with a honey, mustard, and raspberry glaze. Not too difficult. Do you like it, Miss Bea?' We watched her take the first bite, then close her eyes in rapture.

'Mmmm,' was all we could hear, and Derek finally allowed himself a big grin. We feasted that night. Unbelievably, there was still a side dish of rice pilaf, delicately flavored with something citrus – lemon zest, I think – and a dessert that almost brought me to tears. A large pizza pan filled with chocolate chip cookie dough, baked just until the edges were set and the middle still gooey, was placed on the table. Derek had topped this with many scoops of vanilla ice cream, then drizzled the entire concoction with fudge sauce and slivered almonds. We all ate out of that one pan, doing battle for chunks of cookie dough with our spoons.

It was a light-hearted conclusion to a very busy day.

Chapter Five

The morning came extremely early, or at least it seemed that way to me. I had stayed up later than usual, writing a long-overdue letter home to my mother and a few notes to various brothers and cousins. To Neva, I sent a postcard with an old cowboy on the front with a balloon thing coming out of his mouth that said, 'You ain't seen nuttin' yet!' It made absolutely no sense to me, and I knew that was precisely the type of card that would tickle Neva pink. She did have a very wacky sense of humor at times.

Since we had packed the station wagon the night before, there was nothing to do but shower, eat a hasty breakfast, and hit the road. Miss Bea climbed into her customary position as driver, and Derek, who seemed to have an innate compass in his head, took over as Chief Navigator and Map Reader. I sat behind Miss Bea, with LJ crammed in between me and Leslie. For some reason, LJ didn't like sitting near a car door, and since Leslie didn't care for the middle, they were a perfectly matched set.

It really *did* take all kinds to make the world go 'round.

We left our woodsy neighborhood and began the trek to Manchester, Colorado, whose population was 9,035 and growing. A quick check of the Weather Channel had shown today's temperature would be 38 degrees with an overcast sky, which still seemed a bit odd to me. I guess I still measured most places against Piney Woods,

Louisiana. Here, I had on a pair of jeans, an LSU sweatshirt over a long-sleeved T, and a heavy jacket. Back home, I'd have tossed on a pair of shorts and a tank top.

We headed up Highway 25 at a north-eastern angle, according to the map. The aspens that populated the Copper area gave way to spruces and firs, open meadows of golden rod and asters, and a variety of local wildlife. With wild animal experiences not at the top of my list, I wasn't too keen on looking, but the others 'oohed' and 'ahhed' over brief glimpses of deer and squirrels, coyotes, and even a fox or two. I kept my eyes averted, not wanting to add these creatures to my mice and raccoon nightmares.

Around ten o'clock, we pulled into a small town with the name of Big Bertha. For a few minutes I assumed it was some type of a local joke, but the owner of the gas station where we filled up assured me that, yes, this really *was* Big Bertha, Colorado, and it was named for the wife of the mine owner who settled the parts in the mid-1800s.

I knew right then that I needed to replenish my growing collection of postcards to send to Neva, so I purchased a handful. I chuckled to myself as I flipped through them. Neva was going to think that I had gone right over the edge and landed in a Western version of 'Lala Land'.

After a round of bathroom breaks and stocking up on our traveling snacks and drinks, we took off once more. The gas station owner had guaranteed that we would be close to Manchester before three that afternoon. That was fine by me; the skies were looking lower and darker, and I didn't relish the idea of precipitation of any kind at that elevation.

Miss Bea's choice of traveling music was, surprisingly enough, classic rock. I had a brief flashback to when Neva and I were much younger and used to hide in my brothers' rooms listening to their collection of Lynyrd Skynyrd, CCR, and the Rolling Stones. I was impressed by her knowledge of the lyrics as well, and even Derek looked suitably in awe. Leslie had leaned into LJ's massive arm and had begun snoring almost as soon as we were back on the road. LJ was asleep, too, his head bobbing in time to the gentle swerving of Miss Bea's driving.

Surprisingly enough, I was not carsick. Instead, my mind was preoccupied with the performance tomorrow night and with wondering exactly what our accommodation would be like. I had never stayed in a KOA campground before. I had never left home before, at least not this far. And I had never, ever, been away from my mother.

There were a lot of 'nevers' in my life right now, I noticed.

There's a lot to be said for a KOA site. Clean, organized, usually family-friendly, with enough modern amenities to keep even someone like me happy. The place we found ourselves was set just to the south of town, far enough off the main highway to appear isolated, but close enough when a quick ice cream run was called for.

The manager's office resembled a log cabin but, as I approached it, I could see that the 'logs' were actually preformed resin siding, which was a pretty good idea out here in the cold wilderness of northern Colorado. I shivered just thinking about the drafty buildings that people once lived in; definitely not my style, I can assure you.

Percy and Oleta McLaughlin, he tall and slender, she short and plump and a twin for Miss Bea (minus the hair), greeted us with the fervor of long-lost relatives. Before we knew what had hit us, the five of us were settled down into furniture that looked to have been made from random pieces of wood, but was really very comfortable. Mugs of steaming hot chocolate, complete with a snowy dollop of whipped cream, were handed out by Mrs McLaughlin, and Mr McLaughlin followed behind her with a platter of home-made cookies. Apparently Coloradans are as bad – or as good, I should say – as Southerners when it comes to plying guests with food.

I was not going to complain. Neither, I noticed, did anyone else.

I soon discovered the reason for this display of *bonhomie*: our trailers had been let to two other families ('Purely by accident,' said Mr McLaughlin) and could we wait until tomorrow to check in?

No, we most certainly could not, I retorted silently, waiting to hear what Miss Bea would say. To my surprise, she smiled pleasantly, agreeing that it would be no problem at all.

That Miss Bea – always one to pull the proverbial rabbit out. 'I'm sure that you wouldn't mind if we stayed with you overnight,' she suggested, a tad too sweetly. I stifled a laugh. Derek did the same, Leslie stared, and LJ watched Leslie for his cue.

Oleta McLaughlin, perhaps a bit fierier than I had given her credit for, fairly snapped out her answer. They were not, she bristled, the local YMCA. In fact, she noted, that might be the best place for us. 'I'll make a phone call right now,' she offered, turning and walking through the door at the back of the office. I assumed that it led to their private living quarters, the ones Miss Bea wanted to make use of.

Fifteen minutes and much negotiating later (Miss Bea having agreed to bring us back on the morrow in return for one free night and no complaints to the KOA powers that be) we were once again in the wagon and headed out on to the freeway. Thankfully, Derek had thought to ask Mr McLaughlin for the directions, as the two women were still being a bit snippy with one another, so we made it to the Manchester YMCA without a hitch.

It was your typical small town gym and hostel: one large block and stucco building, subdivided inside into the workout areas and the rooms. At least the plumbing was good, and the thought of a long hot shower appealed to me. Hopefully, it appealed to LJ as well; after five hours crammed in next to him, I deduced the boy had forgotten his personal hygiene that morning. Maybe Leslie's olfactory senses were on the fritz, I concluded.

Leslie and I were assigned to slot in with Miss Bea. The room, although strictly utilitarian, was clean, and the bunk bed was a triple-stack, the first one I had ever seen. The boys were just down the hall at the men's end of things – they kept the sexes separate here – although I could still hear them quite clearly. Those two had more bodily noises than my seven brothers put together!

It's safe to say that my rest that night was slightly less restful than I was used to. Miss Bea, I discovered, snored. It was, to be sure, more of a delicate, ladylike snuffle, but I still heard it quite clearly from my perch atop the third bunk. Leslie snored as well, a whistling sort of noise, leaving me the odd woman out in their nocturnal duet. Somehow I managed to get in a few hours of sleep. I was not looking forward to being roommates with my two companions for six more nights.

Breakfast was taken in our rooms. We had stopped at a local grocery the night before, purchasing items that would not require any refrigeration or heating. Hence, I found myself munching on a shiny Gala apple, supplemented with a handful of Swiss cheese-flavored snack crackers. Good enough; I would get something more substantial later. Miss Bea nibbled on a few pieces of Melba toast, no doubt concerned with her girlish figure, and Leslie snapped open a diet cola from the YMCA's vending machine to wash down her own apple and crackers.

Certainly not the level of eating to which we had become accustomed, but "it's an ill wind".

I really had no idea what that particular adage meant, but I remember my Crazy Great-Aunt Opal mumbling those very words whenever anything did not go as planned, which was definitely the case here.

Following our sparse breakfast, we took turns going to the shower. I put on my favorite jeans, another sweatshirt advertising my beloved LSU Tigers, and a pair of high tops. A denim jacket completed my outfit. The local weatherman had promised a sunny day with a high of 50, so I figured if I got too warm during the day, I could just tie my jacket around my waist. Finally, all five of us were ready to rock and roll, and we trooped back out to the faithful station wagon, tossing our overnight bags into the area that would have been the trunk in a smaller vehicle. Miss Bea turned the key, the motor roared into life, and we were off.

Posters announcing the Silverton County Fair were plastered on every available space throughout the town of Manchester. The fairgrounds, we were told, lay to the west of the town itself, replete with a track for racing pigs, a huge barn enclosure for the Future Farmers of America and their contests, a covered area for local art displays, and the ubiquitous barbecue pit. I had discovered that most Coloradans preferred a barbecue to a fish fry, but I supposed it was tribute to the Western roots of the state. When I recalled the fish fries and crawfish boils back home, my mouth watered and I found myself feeling a bit odd. Could I be homesick? No – I was merely reminiscing about the food of my childhood, nothing more.

Shoving the memories firmly back to the place from whence they had sprung, I turned my immediate attention to the town that was Manchester. Tidy sidewalks lined with flower-filled planters and judiciously placed iron benches could be seen everywhere I looked. It appeared that Manchester and messiness did not get along. The stores, while small and generally of the mom-and-pop variety, kept the window presentations tasteful and even the newspaper cases displayed neatly folded daily editions. In short, the entire downtown looked like a movie set, at least in my humble opinion. Piney Woods residents, although neat enough, would have never lasted in such environs.

Derek wandered over to a store window to examine more intently the fair poster neatly taped to the inside of the glass. He gave a low whistle, motioning the rest of us to move in closer.

'Did you see this, Miss Bea? They've given us top billing! We're "Becklaw's Murder Mystery Tour, here for a six-night engagement only! Get your tickets while they last! Entrance to the performance includes a home-made barbecue supper. Drinks extra." That's pretty cool.' Derek looked at Miss Bea, a fond look on his face. 'You've done well, Miss Bea.'

Miss Bea preened, which was certainly her right. I would have, if I had been the one to think this whole thing up, hire four non-actors, and manage to achieve the heady heights of top billing at the Silverton County Fair. I was pretty excited, too, and wondering about the bit-parters that had already been hired for the duration.

My thoughts must have telegraphed themselves to Miss Bea, who looked at all of us and announced that we had a nine o'clock meeting at Skinny Joe's Steakhouse and Brewery. 'To meet the folks I've taken on to help us,' she clarified. I felt relieved, while the boys looked disappointed. It was a bit too early in the day for indulging, I thought.

That gave us enough time to stop at a local restaurant for a hot meal. My toasted English muffin sandwich was absolutely delectable, oozing egg and molten cheese from the sides, the thick piece of Canadian bacon bigger than the muffin itself. A large frosted glass of OJ sat at my elbow, and I alternated between sips of it and my mug of coffee. The cottage fries that came with the sandwich were almost as good as Miss Bea's. Ah. Much better than crackers.

When we had all eaten to our heart's content – well, I know that I had, but I can't speak for LJ, whose appetite seemed endless – we paid the bill and waddled out to the wagon. With a slight groan, I heaved myself into position on the back seat. I hoped I would be hungry enough to enjoy lunch because I had spotted the restaurant's menu and was determined to get back there.

Skinny Joe's Steakhouse and Brewery sat at the juncture of the town's two main streets – a large brick building with a roof of some type of metal that had been formed into fancy shapes. Quite metropolitan for such a small place, I thought to myself, remembering the modern buildings that punctuated the cityscape of Alexandria. I was surprised, then, to see the rough refectory-style tables and benches that marched in lines across the middle of the great space inside. I guess I thought that the interior would match the outside, but there's no accounting for taste, as my mother always says. It was still impressive to a small town girl from Piney Woods, where the biggest building we had was Queen of Peace, the Catholic church, and its adjoining Madonna Hall.

Skinny Joe could have been a member of the Anderson bunch; his name no more matched his build than Sleepy Uncle Pete's did his character. He stood at more than six feet tall, and was about that same distance around. His belly stuck out alarmingly from behind a dirty apron, and the rolls that formed his waist jiggled and bounced with the effort of movement. I found I was holding my breath while watching him teeter toward us, wiping his hands on the apron, a broad smile on an equally broad face.

'Welcome to Manchester, folks,' Skinny Joe announced in a voice that was surprisingly musical and mellow. I guess I expected something rough and gravelly, or high and flighty; that's usually the range for bigger men, I've noticed. 'The young 'uns are on their way, so sit tight. Could I offer you a drink on the house?'

Derek and LJ perked right up, but Miss Bea stepped in and declined, saying that we'd just had breakfast. 'But a nice pot of coffee would be a right treat,' she added, looking around for confirmation. Leslie and I nodded in agreement, while the boys just looked irked.

Skinny Joe rolled back in the direction of the bar, and soon the aroma of freshly brewing coffee filled the air. We settled alongside a table, segregating ourselves, boys on one side, girls on the other. Isn't it funny how even adults still do this? Leslie and I chatted a bit, discussing the various ideas for our roles that we had come up with on the ride up to Manchester from Copper. Derek and LJ sat with their heads on their hands, looking vaguely bored. I guess they thought they needed that drink on the house in order to perk up a bit.

Miss Bea sat silently, gently kneading the meaty part of one hand while her eyes stared at something in the distance. She did this when she was deep in thought, I had noticed. I wondered what she was thinking about then.

Joe came bustling back into the dining room, balancing a large metal tray with six coffee mugs – it was break time for him as well, I guessed – a sugar bowl, a little pitcher of cream, and a carafe of coffee. With a groan, he set the tray in the middle of the table, then heaved his bulk onto the bench beside Leslie.

Someone had forgotten to tell him about the segregation thing.

Chapter Six

The coffee was smooth, and I could tell that the beans were of a higher quality than I usually purchased for myself. The cream was really cream, complete with a bit of foam on top, and the sugar was really sugar. No imposter ingredients for Skinny Joe. That was at odds with my overview of the town itself, but I could have been wrong about that anyway.

We sat and sipped in silence, the aroma of the coffee wafting above our heads as gently as a spring breeze. From somewhere outside, I heard a car door slam, then another. Voices could be heard, and Joe got up to greet the three young men who came noisily into the restaurant.

'Miss Bea, this here's Andy Grimes, Bert Landy, and Julian Sweet. They deal cards at the local casino, so they're perfect for what you've got in mind.' Joe patted the arm of the one called Andy. 'Andy's my brother's kid and I know he'll do right by you. I've known these other two for as long as I can remember. Boys, say howdy to Miss Bea.'

If I didn't know better, I would have thought that even Skinny Joe was trying to get 'into character', as Miss Bea might say. But the three 'boys' didn't seem to notice anything out of the ordinary, so maybe I was wrong about Skinny Joe as well.

'It's nice to meet you, ma'am,' Andy stuck out his hand

and pumped Miss Bea's plump one vigorously. Bert and Julian did the same, and I was fearful that Miss Bea's hair would come tumbling down around her ears with the motion. I didn't carry any hairpins with me, and I was certain that she had already used her entire collection today in her hairdo.

Miss Bea looked them over, a pleased expression on her chubby face. I thought for a minute that she was going to walk around them much like a farmer at a cattle show, but thankfully she restricted herself to a quick look up and down. Probably sizing them up for a costume, I realized. The woman really had a talent for that sort of thing.

'Come sit down and have a cup of coffee with me,' invited Miss Bea, leading the trio over to the table. They lined up on the same side as Joe had; maybe in Manchester, they didn't segregate as much as we did in the South. I saw that LJ's beefy hands had moved across the table toward Leslie, and that the newcomers had spotted it. This seemed to give them the impetus to begin flirting with Leslie while ignoring me, and I could picture the closeness of the cast evaporating into thin air.

Miss Bea picked this up as well, because she suddenly stood up, marched to the end of the table, and directed us to move down toward her 'with the regular actors on my left and the local talent on my right.' We moved as we were told to do, and LJ's face seemed to smooth out a bit as he settled into his accustomed place next to Leslie. Derek sat on the other side of her, and I smiled inwardly. *Our* boys had closed ranks against the intruders.

'All right, we're still waiting on a couple more to get here, but I'll get started with your parts in this.' She nodded at Andy, Bert, and Julian.

She then proceeded to outline the plot of the story, describe their characters and the parts they would play, and talk a bit about what she intended the outcome to be

48

audience participation-wise.

'We've already performed this and have worked out some kinks in the storyline. Hopefully we've gotten them all, but if not, we'll modify as we go. I want the audience to be able to have two or three characters to look at as the murderer; that'll make it a bit tougher to guess, which will keep them interested.' Miss Bea turned to Derek. 'Did you remember to pick up those cigars?'

'Sure did, Miss Bea. I got the cheapest, so they won't be super mellow, but at least we'll have the ambience.' He grinned at the locals. 'Hope you boys smoke.'

'I sure do,' piped up Julian. He was the quietest of the bunch. 'I smoke, too,' added Andy. 'But not Bert here.'

Bert nodded, his face solemn. 'Gave it up three years ago.'

'OK, that's taken care of. Leslie, we got a few more sizes for the local girls, right?' Miss Bea looked down the table at Leslie.

'Yes, Miss Bea. I'm prepared for whatever size ... for all possibilities.' She grinned at me. We were both thinking about that conversation back in Copper.

I was aware of the door opening once more, and looked over my shoulder to see two gals in their mid-twenties or thereabouts walking into the restaurant. Andy jumped up right away.

'Josie. Lily. Nice to see you two. Are you a part of this play as well?' He bussed each young woman's proffered cheek, lingering a bit longer with Josie. Hmm. I wasn't sure that we needed another couple here on the tour with us.

Lily headed for the table, pausing shyly before choosing a spot next to Julian. She had a sweet face graced with brilliant blue eyes, a lipsticked mouth that smiled at each person in turn, and dimples deep enough to sink a finger in. 'I'm so excited to do this, you have no idea!' she exclaimed. 'When Skinny Joe came to the library and told me about this, I couldn't believe my luck.' She beamed at Miss Bea. 'Thanks, ma'am, for letting me join your troupe.'

Miss Bea smiled back. 'Call me Miss Bea, Lily. And I'm delighted that you were able to join us. Leslie, could you take a moment and tell Lily what she'll be doing?'

'Sure thing, Miss Bea.' Leslie got up from the table, motioning Lily to follow. They settled into chairs near the front door, and I could see Leslie rattling on about the part, and Lily's earnest manner as she listened and asked questions.

By this time, Josie had made it over to the table, very much aware of the effect she was having on the male occupants. Her face was as pretty as Lily's but there was something harder in her eyes and in the way she looked each person over. I thought about the different costume sizes that Leslie had chosen and packed, and I sincerely hoped that there would be one to accommodate her, well, extremely ample figure on top.

Miss Bea welcomed Josie to the troupe, introducing her to the others as the 'gal who would play the "lady of the night".' I could see that the menfolk approved of that role. Josie liked it as well, preening her blonde head slightly as she acknowledged Miss Bea's announcement.

We spent the next half hour discussing the storyline, checking and double-checking for obvious holes in the plot. Chuckling, Miss Bea assigned the murderer's role to Julian and that of the victim to Josie.

'I clean forgot to have a murderer in my Murder Mystery Tour last show, so let's get it straight right now, shall we?' We all nodded, wanting this to be an A1 performance of which Miss Bea would be proud. Well, I knew that was the way that LJ, Derek, Leslie, and I felt; it was my fervent desire that these four newcomers would feel the same.

Finally it felt like all bases were covered and that all holes had been plugged. We agreed to meet at the fairground near the front entrance and have a practice that afternoon before the evening's engagement. I could feel the slightest movement of butterfly wings in the pit of my stomach; this audience would be much larger than the one at the Moose Lodge and I didn't want anything to go wrong.

Looking back, I can see that we missed the warning signs right from the get-go.

They were flashing neon bright and none of us, me included, had an inkling of the trouble that would take place before we left Manchester.

But that was all in hindsight, which, as everyone knows, is 20/20.

Amazingly, I was hungry again and ready for lunch. Thankfully, I wasn't the only one who had enjoyed our breakfast, and we loaded up the wagon and headed to the same restaurant.

Lunchtime was a bit more crowded and we had to wait for a table, but we were all perfectly content to do so. The hostess, a college-age girl in a gingham shirt, tight blue jeans, and cowboy boots handed us a menu to browse through so we could order as soon as we were seated. All around us, others were doing the same; who was I to break a local custom?

The menu featured full-color pictures of fruit pies portioned onto thick white china plates, topped *à la mode* or with a slab of cheddar, and thickly cut steaks that had been grilled to perfection, served with loaded baked potatoes or cottage fries, and coleslaw or macaroni salad.

When I think about this time, it is the food that is the most memorable. I had come to Colorado to be an actress and had found Food Heaven.

We were seated next to the large window that looked out over the main thoroughfare. Noontime traffic was in full swing, meaning that a total of six cars were counted as we ate lunch. Foot traffic was much more common, and the neat sidewalks were full of people meandering to lunch dates or to one of the cute little stores that lined the street.

I thoroughly enjoyed my lunch. I had ordered the grilled prawns and scallops on a bed of linguine, the whole thing drizzled in a garlic butter. I could tell it was real butter, too; none of that faintly oily taste that I associate with vegetable spread was apparent. It came with a Caesar salad and garlic breadsticks, and I ate every bite, using my bread to sop up the last of the butter sauce. Delicious!

Once again stuffed to the brim, I silently promised myself to start eating more wisely. What that entailed, I didn't define too clearly, but I figured if I left off the bread and only had butter once a day, I'd be in good shape.

Speaking of shapes, Leslie was having a difficult time matching a dress up with Josie's buxom figure. The bottom of the dress would be fine, but the top was way too tight. Finally, with help from Miss Bea, she decided to have Josie leave the bustier unlaced and add a lacy camisole under it. That was the only possible way to get that girl into anything that looked right for a fallen woman.

Lily was easier to dress. She was slightly built, without the issues that Josie had (a polite way of saying she was flat-chested) and could use any one of the dancer dresses available. Leslie chose to put her in a bright pink number that had cream-colored lace marching down the front and on the short train. The bodice was laced up with pink silk ribbons, and a 'modesty panel' had been added for the reserved Lily. Even if I hadn't known she was a librarian, I would have still guessed that. Or a nanny. She seemed to be one who could coax the most recalcitrant child into behaving. I had watched her at the meeting this morning and was confident that I had pegged her correctly.

That, dear reader, was definitely an error in judgment, as I was eventually to discover.

We made the move from the Manchester YMCA back to the KOA trailers, welcomed with open arms by the McLaughlins. Miss Bea and Mrs McLaughlin were still a bit cautious with one another, but Mr McLaughlin more than made up for his wife, cracking jokes and helping us move our bags into the trailers.

The boys had a two-bedroom affair near the entrance to the park, complete with a barbecue grill and deckchairs. We ladies were put into a three-bedroom mobile home on the edge near the line of spruces that marched next to the campground. It gave me a sense of privacy among the many other trailers parked near us, and I was happy to take the bedroom furthest from the front. I was thrilled to have my own room again, since I was not looking forward to another night of 'bells and whistles' from the two other gals. As much as I had gotten fond of Miss Bea and Leslie, I was fine with not sharing too much personal space with them.

We still had a little while before taking off for the fairgrounds, so I invited Leslie to go on a walk with me. I needed to get out into the open and stretch my limbs, and I also wanted a chance to chat with her outside Miss Bea's keen hearing.

I'd had a funny feeling since that morning, one that I could not put my finger on, and I needed to air the topic from another perspective. I'm not psychic in the least, but I've always had somewhat of a gift, you could say, for discerning the intentions of others.

Someone who had joined our troupe had upset the

emotional balance, and I wasn't sure which it was. Well, that's not precisely true. I had a strong suspicion that Josie was going to be trouble with a capital 'T', and I was fairly certain that I knew what kind of trouble she'd brought with her. What I wasn't sure of was who her 'partner in crime' could be. Andy? He had seemed infatuated with her and had given LJ fits over his flirting with Leslie. To my mind, Julian was out of the running; he was too meek and laid back to cause any problems. The same went for Bert. I saw him as a decent guy, not given to obvious reactions to much of anything, and not one to start a fuss over a girl.

Leslie and I strolled down the path, having called out a farewell to Miss Bea and an assurance that we'd be back in twenty minutes or so. The day was clear and absolutely still; not even the slightest breeze moved the trees and the air was icy. I shivered, tucking deeper inside my sweatshirt and pulling the jacket tighter around me. I liked cold weather, maybe even loved it, but that was when I was snug inside a warm house, feet covered and a good book at hand. The faster we moved, though, the warmer I got, and soon I was able to relax the tight muscles in my back and enjoy the view.

'So what's on your mind?' asked Leslie as we turned right at the office and continued around the campground's perimeter. The McLaughlins had planted beds of flowers native to the area: creamy thistle and blue star, pensternon and Colorado blue columbine, milkweed and cowbane; a lovely mix of whites and blues against the green of the trees. The effect was breathtaking, and I found myself comparing these woods, so cold and clean, to the damp pine forests of Louisiana. I loved my home, but I was becoming quite fond of this new vista as well.

I stopped walking and turned to face Leslie, unsure how to phrase my concern.

'Well?' she asked, adding, 'If you're worried about the

performance, don't. You'll do fine.'

I shook my head.

'No, it's not that at all. I … well, I just don't like the way the mix feels this time around, you know …?' I looked at her earnestly, hoping that she would indeed know what I meant.

'What do you mean, "the way the mix feels this time around"?' It was Leslie's turn to look quizzical. 'Do you mean the local guys? The way they'll portray the characters?'

'No, not that so much as the way everyone responds to each other,' I replied slowly, stooping down to pick a soft Colorado thistle. 'I just felt, I don't know, some strange vibes this morning.'

Leslie laughed, brushing a friendly hand across my shoulders. 'Oh, you mean Josie and the Men.' The way she said it, the word, I could hear the capital 'M'.

'Yes, and no. I'm not making much sense here. I guess I want this whole thing to be as smooth as possible. Miss Bea has worked so hard on this and I'll be damned if I let some outsiders wreck it for her.'

I meant every word.

'Yeah, I know how you feel. She's amazing.' We started walking again, taking the long way back to our trailer. 'I don't want her disappointed either.' Leslie paused. 'I think I'll keep that Josie in my sight at all times. She'd be just the type to cause a ruckus.'

I fervently agreed, although I still harbored a niggling feeling in the back of my mind. I wasn't sure that what I had picked up on could be laid entirely at Josie's pedicured and high-heeled feet.

Miss Bea was in something of a tizzy when we returned to the trailer. Her hair, with normally just a few fingers of it waving about, now resembled an entire hand on top of her head.

'Have either of you seen my handbag?' We both stared at her, then at each other. I had indeed seen it; it was a very large, almost suitcase-size monstrosity and it wasn't easy to lose.

'You had it on your arm when we got here, I'm sure of it,' replied Leslie, forehead crinkled with concentration. 'When we stopped off at the McLaughlins' for the keys, I saw you set it down on the table ...' Her voice trailed off. 'Oh, dear, Miss Bea! Do you think that you left it there? In their office?'

'I'll get down there pronto and check it out, Miss Bea. You stay here with Leslie and, I don't know, search around for it. I'll be back in a flash.' I was as good as my word.

I jumped the steps that led from the front door and broke into a trot. While I was in reasonably good shape, I didn't want pull a hammie or anything so dreadful, so I kept it to a slow run. The office wasn't that far and I arrived in a short amount of time. As I rounded the corner of the *faux* log building, I drew up short: the office's interior was dark, the front door shuttered, and the place deserted.

Not one to shy away from a challenge, I strode around the other side of the office and pounded on the door marked 'Private – Manager's Residence'. It, too, seemed to be empty, but I redoubled the pounding, just in case the two McLaughlins were napping, or eating, or otherwise occupied.

The door to a nearby trailer swung open, revealing a very grumpy woman with the ubiquitous lavender hair. Something clicked in my mind, and I took another look: I could not believe my eyes! It was the chatty old woman from the train, the one whose constant yammering had been outdone only by the screaming children. My jaw nearly dropped to the floor.

'What are you trying to do, young lady?' she barked, glaring at me through a fringe of hair. 'Wake the dead? I am trying to get a nap here.' Apparently she mistook 'napping' for something a little more permanent in nature.

'Oh, sorry, ma'am,' I replied, somewhat intimidated. 'I'm looking for the managers. Did you happen to notice where they went?' I mentally crossed my fingers in the hope that she was as nosey as she was talkative.

She paused, thinking, then shook her head. Another strand of hair fell down. 'I spoke to the wife earlier, but I have seen neither hide nor hair of them since. It was about an hour ago, I'd guess.'

Her eyes seemed to home in on me then, recognition lighting up her powdered and rouged face. 'Aha! I thought I'd seen you before! I remember traveling with you on the train from Piney Woods to Denver. What in heaven's name are you doing here?'

I smiled in what I hoped was a friendly manner, then dipped my head a bit in acknowledgement. 'I came to Colorado – Copper, not Denver – to join Becklaw's Murder Mystery Tour.' I couldn't help it; a tone of pride had crept into my voice and I wanted this old woman to realize that she was in the presence of greatness.

She snorted. 'Becklaw's Murder Mystery Tour'? Don't tell me that you're mixed up with that Beatrice Becklaw!'

I have to confess that I nearly fell over.

Chapter Seven

'Yes – I – Miss Bea …' I could not get out that yes, indeed, I was 'mixed up' with 'that Beatrice Becklaw', and how did she know her? Thankfully, the woman was good at translating stammering lips.

She came fully out of her trailer then, and I noticed that she limped slightly. 'I might have known she would get up to something like this eventually. I'm Lucinda Becklaw, Beatrice's sister-in-law. What is your name, young lady?'

I automatically stuck out my hand. 'Josephine Anderson, ma'am. Jo for short.' We shook, and her grip was certainly firmer than was mine at the moment. I chalked it up to shock.

'Lead the way. I want a word with Beatrice.' Lucinda Becklaw turned and locked the door, then stomped down the porch steps.

I, a survivor of Seven Brothers Boot Camp and not given to questioning my elders, began walking back toward our assigned trailer. I made sure that my gait was slower so that she could easily stay in step. Her limp, more pronounced now that she was moving faster, seemed to fit her, and I noticed with admiration that she didn't rely on anything to help her. I had a feeling that the Becklaw sisters-in-law suited one another.

I went in first. Normally I would hold the door for an

elder and let her precede me into a room, but I wanted to prepare Miss Bea. I owed that much to her, I thought.

Leslie and Miss Bea sat side by side on the trailer's overstuffed couch, Leslie holding Miss Bea's hand and stroking it. I could see that Miss Bea had been crying.

'Ah, Miss Bea,' I began. 'No one was at the office. But …' here I paused, unsure of what to say. 'I ran into someone you might know. May I present Miss Lucinda Becklaw?'

As if on cue, in stamped Lucinda. Also as if on cue, Miss Bea suddenly slumped over, leaning heavily on Leslie's shoulder. Leslie and I exchanged worried looks. Had she fainted? Or worse, had shock sent her heart into a tailspin?

'Oh snap out of it, Beatrice.' Lucinda Becklaw's voice was brusque and she walked over and gave Miss Bea's shoulder a good whack. Miss Bea instantly recovered.

Instead of addressing her sister-in-law, as one might have expected, she turned to me, saying reproachfully, 'Oh, Jo, how could you?'

How could I what? I wanted to ask, but instead kept my peace. Lucinda broke in.

'Still the timid little Beatrice, I can see that clearly,' she said disdainfully. 'Well, it looks as if you need someone around to keep order, and since our dear Desmond has passed on to his reward, may he rest in the peace he never had on earth, it'll have to be me.' She took herself over to one of two armchairs and plopped down heavily, her lame leg sticking straight out in front. It was only then that I noticed the shiny metal of a brace.

Miss Bea sat up straighter, fire in her eyes. 'Oh, no, you won't, Lucy!' Leslie and I looked at her in wonder. We'd never heard such a tone coming from our sweet little Miss Bea.

'Oh, yes, I will, Beatrice, and you will kindly call me by my given name. You know that I detest shortcuts of any kind.' Lucinda gave Miss Bea a hard stare from narrowed eyes, and I shuddered. Old women were worse than children, I was beginning to think.

Leslie had risen to her feet, glancing from one old warrior to the other. 'I could make us some tea, if you'd like, Miss Bea,' she offered. I could tell that she wanted to get away from the shots being launched over the bows of battleships familiar with years of verbal volleying.

'I'll give you a hand,' I stated, not waiting for Miss Bea's reply. 'Leslie, to the kettle.' I guided her out of the front room and through the narrow door into the galley-style kitchen.

Leslie drooped against the counter, arms crossed and a wary look in her eyes. 'Do you think that it was wise bringing that woman here?'

I laughed, a short bark of grim amusement. 'I had no choice in the matter. She just gave me an order and I obeyed. I was afraid not to,' I added, with what I hoped was a pitiful look on my face.

Leslie turned to the cupboard and began pulling out teacups and saucers. 'I suppose they'll be OK in there alone,' she began, hunting now for the tea bags. 'At least I hope so. Do you think that she was close to her brother, what's his name, Dermot?'

'It's Desmond, and I have a feeling that the two of them battled it out for supremacy in Desmond's affections.' I handed Leslie a handful of tea bags; then turned the burner under the stainless steel kettle to 'High'.

'That must be typical behavior for the two of them,' I said, using my chin to indicate the front room where the two old women now sat in complete silence.

With the tea brewed and a plate of store-bought

chocolate chip cookies loaded onto a tray, Leslie and I moved back into the living room. Miss Bea sat with her hands clasped, lips thin and eyes fixed on a point somewhere near the ceiling. Miss Lucinda (that's how I had begun thinking of her) still sat in her armchair, glowering at Miss Bea.

'Here's some tea and cookies,' I announced brightly. 'Miss Bea, Miss Lucinda, would you like one or two?'

'I'll take three,' said Miss Lucinda. 'Give Beatrice one. She's usually watching that figure of hers.' She smirked across at her sister-in-law. 'On second thoughts, I'll take hers, too.'

Miss Bea sat silently, hurt feelings almost palpable. I felt very protective of her just then, and sat down next to her on the sofa. Leslie took the other side, the two of us a buffer from the hurricane that was Lucinda Becklaw.

I tried again. 'So, how are you enjoying your time in Manchester?' I asked Miss Lucinda, who was slurping her tea in a most unladylike manner. Out of the corner of my eye, I noticed Miss Bea's thinly veiled look of disgust.

Miss Lucinda dunked a cookie into her tea and took a bite of the dripping sweet. 'I was doing just fine until this,' she nodded toward Miss Bea, bits of cookie dribbling from the corners of her mouth.

Miss Bea gave a small snort. 'Well, I certainly didn't ask you here, Lucy, as you might recall.' I laughed inwardly; Miss Bea got in an underhanded shot with that 'Lucy' comment.

'Hummph. I can recall many a time when you needed me around, Beatrice. I have a feeling this is one of them.' Another noisy gulp followed this pronouncement. 'So, what exactly is going on?'

'We can't find Miss Bea's handbag, for starters,' I said, reaching out to gently pat the plump hand that lay next to mine.

'OK. That's soon enough sorted. We just need to wait for the McLaughlins to return, as I remember. What's next?' Miss Lucinda's stern glance moved among the three of us, who sat in a line much like naughty children trying to explain ourselves to a strict nanny.

Leslie and I began speaking at the same time, our words tumbling over one another in our haste to assure her that nothing else was amiss.

We didn't convince her.

'I'll be the judge of that, girls,' Miss Lucinda announced. She turned to face her sister-in-law, who instantly cowered closer to me. 'Beatrice, I hear that you've created some foolish mystery tour or some such nonsense. Is that what's causing the ruckus?'

Miss Bea shot to her feet, no easy thing for her to do. She stood as straight as her stature would allow; even her hair seemed to frizzle to a new height, quivering with righteous indignation.

'My Murder Mystery Tour,'– I could clearly detect the capitals – 'is a success, Lucy, and I don't need interference from the likes of you.' She crossed her ample arms over her ample bosom, steam practically billowing from her ears.

Her reaction didn't faze Miss Lucinda in the least. With one last swallow of her crumb-filled tea, she stood to her feet, leaning for a moment on the chair's arm.

'I highly suggest that you begin by being honest with me, Beatrice,' she intoned, heading for the door. 'I will be in my trailer when you are ready to disclose everything. Jo, your arm, if you would.'

Together we descended the steps and began walking back toward the front of the campground. This time she kept a firm grip on my arm, and I had the feeling it was more to detain me than to assist in walking.

'Beatrice has always been a trusting soul.' This declaration, out of the blue, startled me. My mind had been on how to graciously disentangle my arm from hers.

'I would have to agree with that,' I answered, once my heart had shifted from my throat and back to its normal spot in my chest. 'She trusted four complete strangers to come to Colorado and share her home with her.'

In the distance, I spotted Derek and LJ. They were standing near their trailer's front door, watching me approach with Miss Lucinda's grasp firmly on my arm. I decided to take the bull by the horns and steered her gently in their direction.

'Miss Lucinda, there are the other two folks who are part of our troupe. I want you to meet them.'

We approached the boys, Miss Lucinda's limp a bit more pronounced as we walked uphill. We finally reached their trailer, and I lifted my eyebrows in silent warning against any extemporaneous conversation.

At least, I hoped that they understood my meaning.

'Miss Lucinda Becklaw,' – their eyebrows joined mine in the stratosphere – 'this is Derek Robertson and LJ Smythe, the rest of the Murder Mystery Tour troupe.'

Miss Lucinda inclined her lavender head regally, the front part of her hairdo threatening to slip off her head entirely. What *was* it with the Becklaw women and their hair?

'Pleased to meet you, ma'am,' chorused the boys in unison. They looked at me questioningly. 'Is Miss Bea ready to take off for the fairground? We're due to meet up with the bit-parters in forty minutes.'

I slapped my forehead. Dear Lord! I had nearly forgotten the practice, in the excitement of discovering Miss Lucinda Becklaw.

'I'll run and get her right now. No, wait. You go and get her and Leslie, Derek. They're still at our trailer. LJ and I will stay here with Miss Lucinda. Besides, I need to keep my eye on the front office. Miss Bea seems to have left her handbag there, and the McLaughlins aren't answering the door.' I looked over at LJ. 'LJ, you stay here with Miss Lucinda. I'm going to go knock on their door again.' I took off without giving either boy another option.

I once again pounded on the private entrance and this time I had a response. Mr McLaughlin stood in the open doorway, arms firmly folded and a scowl on his face. This cleared the second he saw who it was that stood there; still afraid of bad publicity, I thought.

'Mr McLaughlin, I'm afraid Miss Bea left her handbag in your office. Could I get it for her, please?' I gave him my most charming smile.

'Why, certainly! Let me go around and unlock the office for you.' He stepped out into the sunlight, pulling the door behind him quickly. Maybe Mrs McLaughlin was indisposed.

I followed his lanky frame around the side of the building and to the front door. He inserted a key on a bunch pulled from his pants pocket, holding the door to let me go in first.

I spotted the handbag right away, sitting safely where Miss Bea had placed it that morning. Catching it up, I thanked Mr McLaughlin for his time and left, waving merrily at him.

LJ and Miss Lucinda were exactly where I had left them, in almost the exact same position. LJ's face was a study in misery, and Miss Lucinda looked like she'd eaten a very sour lemon.

Hmm, I thought. Time to institute a little camaraderie here.

'So,' I said, with what I hoped was a natural smile, 'will you be joining us, Miss Lucinda?' I have no idea why I said that; the words seemed to come from somewhere other than the Land of Common Sense.

'I rather think that I will,' she replied, lavender hair bobbing in the light breeze that had sprung up. 'You, young man!' This was directed at a very startled LJ, who stood as straight as he could. I half expected him to salute. 'Go get that good-for-nothing sister-in-law of mine and those other two young people. We have an appointment at the Silverton Country Fairground.'

Somehow we all managed to cram into the station wagon. Miss Bea, still reeling from the shock of having run into her dead husband's sister, drove worse than usual. I was good and carsick by the time we arrived at our destination.

The fairgrounds were set smack dab in the middle of a large, meadow-like area, surrounded by thick stands of spruce and fir trees. For some reason, the locals seemed to have an affinity for faux log buildings, and every structure on the site looked like it had come from the same factory as the McLaughlins' office. We parked near the entrance in the lot reserved for fair employees (I suppose that's what we were), and we hustled off to meet our bit-parters.

The building where the dinner theater would take place was near the center of the grounds; surrounded by low hedges and with flower boxes at the windows, it might well have passed itself off as a private residence.

The huge oak door was propped open with a metal chair. I could hear the sound of voices coming from somewhere inside, talking and laughing with one another. I tried to relax, hoping that the tension I had felt before had dissipated.

I would soon find out that I was wrong. Dead wrong, in a manner of speaking.

Josie sat on a chair near the back of the building, literally surrounded by the Andy, Julian, and Bert contingency. Trying not to be obvious, I glanced around for Lily and finally spotted her sitting alone, head low over the book in her lap. I let out my breath, which I'd been holding without realizing it. That was OK, then. At least there was no verbal sparring going on, no one trying to outdo the other.

They looked up as we entered the darkened hall. Andy sprang to his feet, followed by Bert and Julian. They walked over to meet us, shaking hands with Derek and LJ, and giving the females a friendly nod. They each gave Miss Lucinda a curious glance, but said nothing.

'We're ready to get started, Miss Bea. Just tell us what we need to do to get the place set up,' Andy spoke up, looking eager to please.

Bert nodded. 'Yeah. Just tell us what to do, ma'am.'

Miss Bea looked more energized than she had for the past hour. Turning to look around the spacious room, she pursed her lips as she planned.

Miss Lucinda rolled her eyes.

I leapt into the fray. 'Why don't you have Derek and LJ direct these guys, and Leslie and I will take the gals for some costume fittings?'

Miss Bea gave me a grateful smile. 'That sounds wonderful, Jo. I'll just sit down and go over my notes to make sure that we've got everything together.' She purposefully ignored Miss Lucinda, putting her plump back to her and walking to a nearby table.

Miss Lucinda, not to be outdone, followed me and Leslie as we led the girls for their fittings.

'I'd like a word, Jo,' she announced, not bothering to lower her voice. Miss Bea's head snapped up from her paperwork, an alarmed look on her face.

Chapter Eight

I felt nervous, there was no denying it. The last thing I wanted was to become a pawn in the ongoing Battle of the Becklaw Women. Leslie gave me an apologetic glance, then directed Lily and Josie off to the ladies' room. I stopped walking to let Miss Lucinda catch up, waiting for her to speak.

Lucinda stood still a moment, more to catch her breath than for dramatic pause. In spite of her obvious handicap, this woman was one tough cookie.

'I have decided to join Beatrice in this cockamamie outfit of hers. What job should I do?' She stared at me with eyes that dared me to disagree.

I didn't.

'Well,' I began slowly, 'Miss Bea oversees everything that we do. I suppose you'd better talk to her.' There. I had extricated myself neatly from another Becklaw Pitfall.

Lucinda Becklaw snorted, an almost horsy sound. I fully expected her to lift a hoof and paw the ground in front of us.

'That Woman,' she said, her voice issuing capital letters to the words, 'is a dingbat.'

I had to quickly stifle a grin. I hadn't heard that epithet since watching reruns of *All in the Family*.

'I'm sorry, dearest Lucy?' The words were laden with

sugary sweetness, the voice unrecognizable to me for its dangerously mellow tone. 'I'm afraid I missed that last comment.' Miss Bea had walked up behind me, laying a hand on my shoulder. 'Jo, dear, run along and give Leslie a hand, won't you?'

I obeyed. Quickly.

I scampered down the hall and didn't look back. I don't know what I was afraid of seeing: perhaps my beloved Miss Bea with claws in place of hands and fire issuing from her kindly mouth. I knew that was just a fancy but, from what I had just heard, it could have happened.

Leslie was kneeling down in front of Lily when I walked in, pins bristling from her mouth in a parody of teeth.

'Hng n a minit,' she said, trying to speak without swallowing one of the little daggers.

I looked around the small dressing area. Dresses with lace flounces and feather boas covered nearly every surface. The mirrored dressing table and the cushioned stool that stood in front of it, carried a load of acting minutiae; vials of thick stage make-up and jars of face cream were side by side with all manner of undergarments; push-up brassières and double-sided tape, along with girdles in all sizes, lay strewn around for everyone and their grandma to see.

With Lily's dress reconstructed to her satisfaction, Leslie came groaningly to her feet.

'That carpet needs some new padding,' she grumbled. 'Where's Miss Bea, Jo? I need her to see Lily's dress before I make the changes for tonight.' She bent down and plucked a box of straight pins off the floor.

'Oh, I think that I'd trust your judgment on this one, Leslie,' I said, cutting my eyes sideways at Lily to indicate 'not in front of the newbie, Leslie'.

She didn't get it and babbled on. 'I was just saying to

Lily and Josie that Miss Bea is in the head honcho for everything we do in Becklaw's, isn't that right, Jo?'

What was it with everyone trying conversationally to entrap me today?

I didn't have to answer, thank goodness. We three heard the sounds of rapid footsteps coming toward us. The door was flung open and in stepped Miss Bea, flames figuratively shooting from her eyes. Instinctively, I moved nearer to Leslie and Lily. I don't why I did; Miss Bea wasn't the type to murder me in my tracks ... was she?

'I have just been informed by my dear sister-in-law that she intends to join our little family and run part of the troupe.' Miss Bea's face was unnaturally red, and her hair had completely come undone, its tangled frizzle hanging around her face *à la* Medusa. If that didn't give one nightmares, then nothing could, I thought, as I edged even closer to Leslie.

'What's going on?' Leslie looked from me to Miss Bea, concern evident in her tone. 'Do you need us to run her off, Miss Bea? I can certainly do it and LJ will be more than happy to take care of business for you.'

Miss Bea brushed aside an armful of clothing and plopped down on the stool. I held my breath, praying silently for its safety and hoping that the craftsman had counted on bottoms of all sizes.

'No, that's very kind of you, my dear,' she said, her face less flushed and her voice quieter. 'When I married my sweet Desmond, I essentially married his family. His sisters, Lucinda and Miranda, were so clingy, and his mother, God rest her soul, acted like Desmond wasn't old enough to leave home. We took off as soon as we had the money, leaving kith and kin behind and happy to do it.' She paused, smiling at the ceiling in a way that I now associated with her many visits to a happier past.

'There are two of them?' I couldn't keep the horror out

of my voice, looking back over my shoulder as if another Becklaw Person was going to come swooping at me from the shadows.

'Yes,' smiled Miss Bea in amusement. 'Lucinda and Miranda – Lucy and Mindy – are twins. For every bad point that is Lucy, Mindy is as sweet and kind as the day is long.'

I shook my head in disbelief. I couldn't get out of my head the fact that Miss Lucinda had a twin and that this twin was sweet. 'Sweet' was not an appellation that one would ever, ever apply to Lucinda Becklaw.

Leslie came to life, pointed to Lily's dress, and asked if it looked OK. Miss Bea turned an appraising eye toward the flounces that Leslie had pinned up to accommodate Lily's shorter stature.

'That looks fine, my dear,' Miss Bea said, rising from the stool. I heard a groan and wondered if the stool was thanking its lucky stars that she had stood up.

Once more, the door was opened with force. Miss Lucinda stood there in the open doorway, arms firmly crossed and a stern look on her face. She homed in on Miss Bea, who seemed to suddenly grow ten feet taller and shoot sparks.

'I believe that the actors' dressing rooms are off-limits to the public,' Miss Bea announced in stentorian tones.

'Oh, give it a rest, Bea!' Miss Lucinda bit her words off as cleanly as a seamstress cutting thread.

Leslie turned to look at me, making a slight pointing motion with her head, first toward Miss Bea then toward Miss Lucinda. I shrugged, wiggling my eyebrows to telegraph my opinion. Miss Bea's radar, though, was in fine working order.

'Girls, you don't need to do that,' she admonished sternly, although I swear I could detect a smile in her eyes. 'Whatever it is you need to say, just say it.'

I took a deep breath. Leslie was counting on me to be the leader, and poor Lily was in something like shock, watching the drama unfolding in front of her.

'Miss Bea, Miss Lucy,' I began, then swiftly corrected myself. 'Miss Lucinda. We need to get these costumes ready to go for tonight. Which one of you will be in charge of that?'

I felt the air thicken as Miss Bea's eyes narrowed. I had really stepped in it.

'I am the One in Charge,' Miss Bea said stiffly. I felt crushed. Miss Bea had never used that tone with me.

'I didn't mean it like that, Miss Bea,' I replied contritely. It must have worked, because her sunny smile returned and I felt forgiven. 'What I really meant to say was, are these changes that Leslie made OK with you?' I had clean forgotten that she'd already told us that they were. I was pretty shaken up, I guess.

Apparently she was shaken a bit as well, because she answered, 'I'll take a look in a few minutes, dear. Let me just escort dear Lucy here to the front room first, then we'll go over the costumes. Lucinda?'

Here she opened the dressing room door, holding out her left arm in a magnificently sweeping gesture that said very clearly, Get Out.

Dear Lucy got out.

In spite of the bad vibes between the two Becklaw gals, we managed to fit both Lily and Josie, as well as the Three Amigos. With the clothing issues out of the way, we set about getting the eating area in order, our 'stage' zone defined by a long table (Derek's bar), an upright piano, and three round tables with mismatched chairs. Since we really didn't use props other than the cards, ashtrays, and a few bottles for the bar, we were ready to go.

'Miss Bea,' questioned Josie, 'when I leave to go rest during the play, which direction should I walk?'

As we had already gone over what 'stage right' and 'stage left' meant, I waited for Miss Bea to reply using one of those terms. To my amazement – and amusement – she said, 'You go to your right, Josie, as if you were looking out at the audience and decided to run back to the dressing room. Does that make sense?'

Her tone was kind, not facetious in any way. I could tell then that Miss Bea associated 'beauty' with 'empty head'. Well, who didn't? Josie didn't seem to notice anything of the kind, instead pausing to crinkle her smooth brow, look out at where the audience would be, back to her right, and then nod.

Eureka, I thought. She's got it! (Never mind that I was feeling a bit cynical at this moment, dear reader. I was actually impressed that the girl knew her right hand from her left.) With that little issue taken care of, Miss Bea gave us all last-minute chores to do before we left.

I soon found myself side by side with Miss Lucinda, moving chairs closer to the tables in order to form more walking space for when Leslie and I would venture out among the diners and encourage them to participate. Much to my surprise and thankfulness, she had nothing to say. Instead, she marched up and down to the best of her ability, shoving in chairs with enough vigor to make me think that she still was a bit miffed over the 'Get Out' scene with Miss Bea.

I have to say that right about then I was starting to get a funny feeling about the entire thing: the venue we'd been hired on to play, the way Miss Lucinda showed up out of the blue, and even the way that Skinny Joe insisted on helping to choose the bit-parters. Something Did Not Feel Right. No siree, Bob.

I did have a sort of reputation already, though, as one

who tended to leap to conclusions and even quicker to action, so I was loath to mention any of my gut reactions to anyone. That is, until I was cornered by Miss Lucinda at the end of one of the long tables.

'So spill it already, missy,' Miss Lucinda barked, blocking my path with her girth.

As is my wont, I feigned a look of innocence as my mind raced to decide what I could say to this woman. 'I'm afraid that I don't …' I began, but Miss Lucinda's laser beam glare blew my words clean out of this galaxy.

'Do not play ingenuous with me, young lady! I've had plenty of experience with folks like you who like to think that age dulls one's senses. Well, I wasn't born yesterday,' – a sharp look from her stopped my grin in its tracks – 'so you'd better give it up. Now.'

She sounded a lot like my third grade teacher, scary Mrs Fiornelli with the moustache.

I gave it up.

'Miss Lucinda,' I said, 'I really have a bad feeling about all of this.' There. I'd said it. She could take it or leave it. I hoped she'd leave it.

She took it.

Miss Lucinda plopped down a bit unsteadily, her braced leg stuck straight out in front. She motioned to me to sit down as well, which I did, afraid to defy her.

She really did remind me of Mrs Fiornelli, moustache and all.

As I sat in silence, hoping that I could use this as a defense, Miss Lucinda cleared her throat with a loud 'harrumph', then began to speak.

'I have to admit, Jo, that my finding you all was no accident. I have been concerned for a while about how my brother, well, about his death, its suddenness and the fact that we never saw a body or had a funeral. We've only had

Beatrice's word all these years.' She stopped speaking, staring past me at some memory. She sighed, shaking her head as if to rejoin the real world.

'When our mother passed away, my sister and I promised each other that we'd find out the truth of the matter, no matter how awful or how mundane. If it was true that he'd died in a boating accident and was never found, so be it. But if we found out that Beatrice or someone else had a hand in his disappearance, there would be hell to pay.

'Unfortunately, my sister has also passed, leaving me the sole survivor of the Becklaw family. It's up to me to find out the truth about Desmond and to reclaim anything that might still be rightfully our family's.' She stopped speaking, head down. I felt a wave of sadness for this woman whose entire family was gone, who was left with a nutter like Miss Bea.

Wait a doggone minute, I mentally scolded myself. You just accused Miss Bea, sweet, kind, do-anything-for-anyone Miss Bea, of being as off her rocker as Crazy Great-Aunt Opal.

Well, that stood to reason, didn't it? I knew the symptoms. I suppose I'd known all along that Miss Beatrice Becklaw, Proprietor of Becklaw's Murder Mystery Tour, was a nut. Oh, boy. Where did that leave me? I guess I knew this entire escapade was too good to be true. The best thing for me, I thought wretchedly, was to get myself back to Copper, pack my belongings, and head back to Piney Woods.

Or not. I couldn't just up and leave Leslie to Miss Bea's mercies. Or LJ. Or Derek. Or even Miss Lucinda, for that matter. I was going to have to stick it out, maybe give Miss Lucinda a hand with her investigation. Lord only knew what we'd uncover.

But I was ready. I lifted my head, looked Lucinda

Becklaw straight in the eyes and said, 'You can count on me, Miss Lucinda.'

If I had known what those seven words held in store for me, I would've sooner bitten my tongue than utter them.

Chapter Nine

The rest of the day flew by on butterfly wings. That made perfect sense to me, since the butterflies were back in force in my stomach. I noticed Leslie was a little more subdued than usual, and that LJ was quiet as well, but that was par for the course for him. Derek alone seemed untouched by the nervous fingers of performance anxiety, and I was a tad jealous. And irritated. I was peeved that he seemed so rock-steady when it came to situations that would send the normal heart racing into overdrive while mine did everything but leap straight out of my chest.

Oh well, I consoled myself. Karma would bite him in the butt one day. I just wanted it to be sooner rather than later so I could witness it.

We had returned to the KOA and the sanctity of our respective trailers in order to 'rest our eyes', as my mother always says. I don't know how much 'resting' the others' eyes got, but mine certainly were lacking in that department. I played the conversation with Miss Lucinda over and over in my head, rethinking my decision to stay. I have to admit that I was thoroughly torn.

I had just convinced myself to pack it in when a knock sounded on my door. With a grumble obvious in my tone, I said, 'It's open.' I was not up to receiving visitors the way I was currently feeling.

Leslie's worried face peeked around the corner of the

open door, hesitating for a moment before coming inside all the way. I guess my tone threw her off; I'm not normally the group grump.

'Er, Jo? You got a minute?' She sounded a bit anxious, so I sighed, sat up, and patted the bed next to me.

'Have a sit, Leslie. What's on your mind?' I needed to get switched into Miss Jo's persona anyway.

She sat where I indicated but didn't say anything right away. That was OK. I needed a moment to get my own thoughts together. When she finally opened her mouth, what came out startled me to no end.

'Jo, I'm pretty sure that there's something up with Miss Bea and Miss Lucinda.' She looked at me with trusting eyes, waiting for me to reassure her that, no, indeedy, nothing was the matter and why in the world was she even thinking like that?

I looked back at her, then asked, 'What's made you think that, Leslie?' I wanted to hear her take on matters, to see if it matched my own concerns.

I think that I astonished her. It astonished me, sitting here and talking about Miss Bea as if she was some sort of monster. Which she might just be, at least according to Miss Lucinda.

'I am so worried about Miss Bea,' Leslie began, her voice hesitant, maybe doubting her own intuition. 'That Lucinda Becklaw is up to no good.'

Now it was my turn to be silent. For the life of me, I couldn't think of a suitable response. I had been so geared up to hear something about how Miss Bea was turning out to be a reincarnation of Mrs Fiornelli that I hadn't stop to think that Miss Lucinda might, indeed, be the bad one here, out to harm our sweet Miss Bea (she had already assumed her former label in my mind) and ruin our troupe.

Thankfully my tongue recovers quickly.

'Now, Leslie,' I said, giving my mind time to catch up to my mouth. 'Now Leslie,' I repeated, 'what makes you think that Miss Lucinda is up to no good?' This I had to hear.

Now it was Leslie's turn to be tongue-tied. That condition sure was catching.

'I'm not sure why I even think that,' she finally said, one hand picking at a loose thread on my bedspread. 'There's just something – well, the woman just strikes me as being a bit underhanded.' She said that last part with her chin slightly lifted as if she expected me to give her an argument. Instead, I said nothing, just nodded slowly.

'You think so too?' Leslie's voice had raised a pitch or two, and I quickly leaned over to shush her, pointing with my free hand toward the direction of the living room. Miss Bea's door had opened very quietly, but my ears had caught the dragging sound as the badly hung door moved across the carpet.

We both sat quietly for a moment then both began to speak at once, talking in an overly-cheery manner about the evening's performance. When I was sure that she had gone back to her room and closed the door, I spoke:

'Look, Leslie, we can't go around suspecting old women of anything except maybe cheating at bingo.' I spoke in what I hoped was a tone of assurance, but I still had the niggling doubts in my mind – and now they had doubled. Good Lord, I thought. What in the world have I gotten myself into?

I reached over and gave Leslie's hand a reassuring pat. 'Let's just forget this for the time being and survive this first performance. If you're still feeling this way tomorrow, let's talk about it again. Maybe even with Derek and LJ, just to get a guy's perspective. It might just be us.'

Leslie smiled at me. 'You know exactly how to make

me feel better, Jo,' she said, leaning over and giving me a quick squeeze.

I smiled in what I hoped was a positive manner. I had never felt more negative vibes in my entire life. Well, except for the time I had to spend the afternoon with Crazy Great-Aunt Opal, cleaning out her sewing basket and listening to her stories about 'life on the inside', as she called her assisted-living luxury apartment.

Other than that, life was peachy.

Before I knew it, it was time to hit the road and scoot on over to the Silverton County Fairgrounds. Miss Bea's driving was a bit more erratic than usual, but that might have just been director's jitters. I fervently hoped that was it.

Be that as it may, we eventually arrived in one piece, parking the station wagon alongside the vehicles that belonged to the fair employees. Derek had remembered to grab the orange placard that said 'Silverton County Fairgrounds Employee' on it. He laid it on the dashboard and away we went to face our audience and our fears.

The dining area was already hopping. People were walking through the food line, filling plates with pulled pork or pieces of barbecued chicken, coleslaw and ears of com, baked beans, and rolls. The desserts sat off to the side, next to the table that held four large urns of coffee and half a dozen pitchers of iced water. I took the long way round the room before heading back to the dressing area; I wanted an 'up close and personal' view of the goodies.

Leslie had already changed into her dancing girl costume, topped off with a frothy feather boa slung over her left shoulder and around her neck, by the time I got to the dressing room. I thought the look was perfect; Leslie exuded 'cheap' like a professional.

And I mean that in the nicest possible way.

Miss Bea was helping Lily wriggle into her gear, pulling down on the 'modesty panel' to show a bit more of Lily than Lily was willing to show. As quickly as Miss Bea let the front of the dress go, Lily would tug it back up again. If I didn't have to get ready myself, I would have stood there to see who would win. My money was on Miss Bea.

Josie wasn't there yet, and I saw that Leslie kept glancing at the clock that hung on the wall above the door. There was still enough time, I thought idly. If we all were ready too soon, we'd just set around and make each other nervous. And crazy.

'Crazy' reminded me of Crazy Great-Aunt Opal, which in turn reminded me of Miss Lucinda. Oh, dear. What was it that had my thoughts making that direct connection? I'd just have to tuck this into the back of my mind and let it stew around a while. Eventually it would come to me, I was sure.

I opened the box that held my 'school marm' dress and those killer buttonhook boots and took myself off to a corner to get dressed. I wasn't modest by anyone's standard, that much was true, but I didn't want to give Miss Bea another costume to fiddle with. It was safer if I got out of her way. Hence the corner.

I had bent down to fasten those insufferable buttons when I noticed Leslie and Miss Bea in a worried consultation. It was probably about that Josie again and, come to think of it, she probably should have been here ten minutes ago. That was a pet peeve of mine; being 'fashionably late' was not my idea of polite behavior. Well, she'd better be on her toes when she arrived or Miss Bea would take her pay out of her pretty little hide.

A knock at the door caused all three of us to jump.

Leslie called out, 'Who is it?'

I strained my ears to see if I could hear Josie's tinkly little laugh, which, by the way, was pet peeve number two. So far she had two of the five things that bugged me, and that did not bode well for her in my book.

'Miss Bea? Miss Lucinda sent us to fetch you.' Andy – or Bert, or maybe it was Julian – was on the other side of the door. Miss Bea wrenched it open in one mighty tug. Leslie and I looked at each other in surprise; as my brothers would say, 'Who'da thunk it?' Miss Bea was certainly full of surprises.

'And just what does That Woman want?' Miss Bea's voice fairly dripped with scorn. I saw Bert flinch (it was Bert out there) and take one step back as if to create a buffer between him and the small dragon he now saw standing in front of him.

'Ah, ma' am, she just said that you needed to get out to the parking lot as soon as possible.' Bert looked unhappy at having to deliver an order to Miss Bea. I couldn't say that I blamed him one iota.

'Oh. She. Did.' Miss Bea's words were so clipped that they formed their own sentences, complete with punctuation. Heaven help Miss Lucinda if this wasn't a true emergency, I thought wryly.

'Yes, ma'am. I can take you to her if you'd like, ma'am.' Poor Bert. I could tell that he wanted to be as far away from Miss Bea as was humanly possible, but this boy's mama had raised him right. Kudos to her, whoever she was.

I decided to relieve him of his duties.

'I'll handle this, Bert,' I replied kindly, reaching out and giving his arm a tiny shove in the guise of patting him. The shove said 'get as far away as possible', and he took the hint.

More kudos to his mother, may God bless her. She had trained him to be woman-ready, radar and all.

He hustled out of there as fast as his polite little legs could take him. I turned to Miss Bea and Leslie and said, 'Shall we?' as I motioned toward the hall with a sweeping gesture. I do so love a good drama, and this certainly had all the makings of one. Lily made no move to join us, and I didn't insist.

I guess I half expected that Miss Lucinda would actually be waiting for us inside but there was no sign of her as we entered the main eating area and paused to scan the room. I shrugged, lifting an eyebrow as I looked at Leslie. She gave a half-shrug back and nodded. I turned to Miss Bea, taking her plump elbow in my hand.

'I can run ahead and see what she wants, or we can all go together. Which suits you, Miss Bea?' I mentally voted on the first option. I wanted to get the scoop first and get Miss Lucinda calmed down if I needed to.

'Don't be silly, child.' Miss Bea smiled up at me, but her eyes were battle-ready. 'I will not leave you to fight my skirmishes without my support. Onward and upward, girls!'

I swear I could hear the sound of bugles and smell the acrid scent of gunpowder.

Chapter Ten

With Miss Bea leading the way, we three marched out to the parking lot. I actually did feel quite militant, although I suspected we simply looked like three nutty women off to rein in a recalcitrant husband or boyfriend. Oh, well, I sighed inwardly. No one from Piney Woods could see me and tell my mom that I was getting more and more like Crazy Great-Aunt Opal by the day. That was, at least, some relief.

It was also the last relief I was to have for some time after that.

To our surprise, the parking lot was alight with the flashing blues and reds of police and emergency vehicles. I heard Miss Bea moan, 'Not my car, oh please, not my beautiful car!' I almost laughed aloud.

A ribbon of yellow crime scene tape fluttered in the evening breeze and I shivered in my thin dress. I stole a glance at Leslie, who had scooped up a jacket just as we left the dressing room. Smart move on her part, I acknowledged. It kept her warm and let the men's eyeballs stay in their heads where they belonged. I would have hated to see Miss Bea go ballistic over some silly men.

I spotted Miss Lucinda standing off to one side of the scene in front of us, a tall man in a police uniform standing near her and writing something down. Oh, dear Lord, I thought with alarm. Miss Lucinda's gone and bashed in Miss Bea's precious vehicle!

It would have been much, much better if it had been that silly old car.

I don't know if I actually noticed Josie first, or if Miss Bea did. All I can recall is that suddenly the two of us were through the yellow tape and staring down in horror at the tiny, twisted body of Josie, her hands flung up above her head as if in flight and a hole in her chest. I prayed that it had been a quick journey.

'Er ... ma'am?' With a quick look at his paperwork, the officer who had been talking to Miss Lucinda approached us. 'Are you Beatrice Becklaw of Becklaw's Murder Mystery Tours?' Something in his tone alerted me and I stepped forward without thinking; which is another one of my specialties.

'Yes, this is Miss Bea, and before you ask it, we have never, ever had a real live dead body in one of our performances.' I could have crawled under a rock as soon as the words left my mouth. "A real live dead body"? Really, Jo?

His eyes flashed in my direction briefly, and thankfully I saw a glint of amusement there. 'Ma'am, I just need to speak with Beatrice, with Miss Bea here, so if you'll wait over there by'– his hand gestured toward Miss Lucinda, who was staring at poor Josie with a look of complete sadness on her face.

'Sure.' I said hurriedly. I grabbed Leslie by the jacket sleeve and walked over to where Miss Lucinda stood.

'What in the world?' I hissed at Miss Lucinda, not wanting to be overheard by the gathering crowd of Nosey Nellies.

She turned her eyes toward me, and I was again struck

by the depth of sorrow I saw there.

'I needed to run out to the car to grab a bag Derek had forgotten, and there she was.' she said simply, turning back to nod at Josie. 'I gave her a shake but I could tell she was already gone. Poor little girl.' The words came out softly, mournfully, and I felt compelled to put my arm around her.

The feelings from earlier came back to me, and I could tell by the way that Leslie was looking at me that she remembered them as well. Great. Now I would not only be known as a crazed psycho who attracts killer animals but also as a psychic, who could predict the future. The Psycho Psychic.

I had to admit it, though; it did have a bit of a ring to it.

'Jo?' Leslie was tugging on my sleeve, pulling me back to the present. 'Miss Lucinda asked you a question.'

'I'm sorry, Miss Lucinda,' I said. 'What did you say?'

'Where was Beatrice about twenty minutes ago? Was she with you?' Her eyes bored into mine, her words heavy with meaning. I literally jumped back from her, anger building rapidly.

'I don't know what you are implying,' I spluttered, but Miss Lucinda placed a placating hand on my arm.

'I'm not implying anything, Jo,' she said, her voice suddenly gentle. 'I just don't want her interrogated unnecessarily. She isn't a strong person, you know.'

I think that I did know that already, although Miss Bea could fake 'strong' better than anyone I had come across.

'Well,' I began, turning to look at Leslie. 'We got here and went to the dressing rooms right away ...' My voice trailed off and I looked at Leslie. 'Actually,' I said slowly, 'I walked around the dining room first, looking at the food and especially at the dessert table. Leslie, you and Miss

Bea walked ahead of me, so you two went to the room first.'

It was Leslie's turn to squirm. 'Ah, actually, I had to run to the little girls' room, so Miss Bea went on ahead of me as well.' She gave a little shrug. 'I didn't know something like this was going to happen.'

'No one did, Leslie. Except for the killer,' I added hastily. 'Which I am sure is not Miss Bea, by the way.' I stared at Miss Lucinda somewhat defiantly, daring her to contradict me.

'Well, I happen to agree with you, Jo,' said Miss Lucinda to my surprise. 'I personally don't think that Beatrice has a murdering bone in her body.' Aha! I latched on to that statement *tout de suite,* as the French say.

'Oh, really, Miss Lucinda?' I made my voice as sweet as pie. 'Then she couldn't have had anything to do with Desmond's death?' I had trapped her but good and she knew it.

Miss Lucinda, bless her heart, had the grace to blush. I think it was then that I decided that I liked her almost as much as I liked Miss Bea.

'All right,' she said with aplomb. 'Maybe I was a bit hasty in my estimation of Beatrice.' She turned around and looked at where said Beatrice was standing. 'I suppose I wanted to track her down just for the sake of seeing her again.' She sounded almost wistful.

Man, these Becklaw women were cool customers, I thought admiringly. I, too, turned to look at Miss Bea. Back straight, head high, shoulders back. She truly was a warrior, ready to fight for whoever needed her. I was glad she was in my corner.

'I think that we should say something to the officer, you know, something that may help Miss Bea out of whatever it is she's accused of.'

I wish that I had kept my trap shut. Leslie's eyes were instantly as huge as the proverbial deer in the headlights, and Miss Lucinda gave my arm a sharp jab with a boney finger.

'We don't know that she's being accused of anything, Jo,' admonished Miss Lucinda. 'I'd thank you to keep your gob shut and use your brain.' She began walking back toward the officer and Miss Bea, an air of determination in her step.

I ran to catch up with her, and Leslie hurried to join us.

'I just couldn't stay back there with the ... you know, by the ...' She gulped, unwilling to bring herself to say the word. Being the soul of kindness that I am, I finished the sentence for her.

'The body? Well, who would?' I looked over Miss Lucinda's shoulder at a distraught Miss Bea.

'What do you think that officer is saying to her?' murmured Leslie in my ear.

'I have not a clue,' I whispered back. Miss Bea's head suddenly swiveled, looking straight at us. I groaned. That woman's hearing was right up there with a bat's.

I moved closer to Miss Lucinda's broad back. She had not said anything yet, but I could feel the air around her go still. It was weird, to say the least.

Miss Lucinda was going into attack mode.

'If my sister has not been charged with anything, officer, I'd thank you to wrap it up and let her get back inside. The poor dearie is in a state of shock.' She moved forward to place a large arm around Miss Bea's shoulders.

Actually, it was Leslie and I who were in shock – "My sister?" – "Poor dearie?"– Dear Lord, what was this world coming to?

The officer must have realized his perilous position, facing the Becklaw Wall of Sisterhood. He did what any other red-blooded man would have done: he snapped closed his notebook, took a step back, touched his forehead in something akin to a salute, and wished us all a good evening.

As he walked back to his *compadres*, an awkward silence settled over the four of us like a blanket; oddly enough it was somewhat comforting. We all began to move at once, Leslie and me flanking Miss Lucinda as Miss Bea's bodyguards. I didn't mind getting drilled by what felt like sixty pairs of eyes as we made our way back to the safety of the dining hall, but I was danged if I was going to let anyone bother Miss Bea.

Chapter Eleven

The 'powers that be' had cleared the dining area, setting it up as a command post for the local police department and the paramedics to work. Miss Bea was definitely suffering from shock, and a young woman in an Emergency Medical Tech's uniform came over and met us at the door, gently drawing Miss Bea from the protective grasp of Miss Lucinda.

We three stood in silence, watching the bustle around us. Two officers had commandeered a long table and had placed a chair directly across from theirs; I guessed that's where the suspects would sit.

'We'll have to talk to those officers,' I said out of the corner of my mouth to Leslie and Miss Lucinda. 'I have no idea what they'll ask me, though; I haven't seen Josie since earlier today.'

'None of us have, Jo,' said Miss Lucinda, giving me another laser look, a few seconds before sweeping the full beam of her glare around the room. 'Just what they hope to gain from this nonsense, I'm sure I don't know. Well, I'm going to get this over with.' And with that, she marched over to the table, plopping her heft onto one of the chairs.

Pushing back a lock of lavender hair from her forehead, Miss Lucinda looked sternly at the officer across from her. I grinned, feeling slightly sorry for that young man. He was about to unleash the Becklaw Barrage. I hoped he'd had his Wheaties.

Leslie elbowed me in the side. 'Look!' she hissed. 'There's that guy from the steakhouse, that Scrawny Joe or whatever it is he called himself.' She pointed unobtrusively with her chin at the rather large individual who filled the open doorway.

'What's *he* here for?' I wondered aloud, watching him walk over to one of the paramedics and say something. He must have asked where someone was, because I saw the EMT look over his shoulder, then point. Skinny Joe nodded briefly and walked away, his bulk following a course of its own.

'Hey, wait a minute,' I exclaimed. 'He's heading for the dressing rooms, Leslie. Let's follow him and see what he's up to.' I spun on my heels and took off without a backward glance, trusting that Leslie was following me.

Together we walked down the hallway, pausing briefly in front of the women's dressing room. I put my ear to the door but could hear nothing, so I motioned to Leslie to move on. We turned the corner and saw that the door to the men's dressing area was ajar. I could hear a murmur from inside and I stopped in my tracks, very nearly sending Leslie over in a heap.

I cut my eyes toward the door, then back at her, putting my finger to my lips. I began moving along the wall *a là* Super Secret Agent, and almost ran right into Joe's hefty belly. I tilted my head and looked up into his eyes. He did not look happy to see me, not one bit.

'Ah, hello there, Mr Skinny. Mr Joe.' What a complete idiot, I thought, my traitor of a flush creeping above the high collar of my 'school marm' dress. I felt dumb, but defiantly so. I returned his look, glare for glare.

'I take it you're here for a reason?' Leslie's quiet voice sounded from behind my right shoulder where she had taken refuge from Skinny Joe. Oh, how brave we can be when hunkered down behind somebody else! I had to admire her pluck, though.

'I'm here to pick up my nephew. What's your excuse?' With his beefy arms folded against a massive chest, Joe looked like an illustration of the Jolly Green Giant, only without the jolly. Or the green. He looked, in a word, annoyed.

'We,' – I indicated Leslie with a thumb jabbed in her direction – 'are here to tell the boys that they're wanted out front.' Since this was a flat out lie, I didn't chance a look in Leslie's direction. That girl was too truthful for her own good.

I could see Skinny Joe's mind turning this bit of information over. Thankfully he bought it, and stuck his head back in the door and called out, 'Andy! Bert! You two get out here. You're wanted out front.' He turned to face me, arms still crossed. 'There. Satisfied?'

'Yes. Yes, we are. Come on, Jo. We still need to round up Lily.' Leslie grasped me by the back of my dress and all but hauled me bodily down the passageway.

'Hey,' I began, but she tugged me further down the hall before stopping and hissing in my ear, 'I think he's in on it!'

'Who's in on what?' I was stymied. I couldn't think of a rational thing to say, so just stood and stared at her. We could hear the footsteps of Andy and Bert moving at a rapid pace behind us, so we hightailed it into the dining area/police substation and walked over to where Miss Lucinda was still keeping watch over Miss Bea.

Thankfully, Miss Bea's color was almost normal now, and the faint sheen of sweat that had covered her forehead was gone. Someone had brought her a glass of water and she sat sipping it quietly, not looking at anything in particular. Miss Lucinda's hands were on Miss Bea's shoulders, gently patting them.

I think that this qualified as "a cold day in Hades".

Leslie and I both turned to watch as Andy and Bert, followed by Skinny Joe, stopped just inside the dining area. They looked around in a puzzled manner, their eyes lighting on us.

'Just follow my lead,' I said to Leslie from the side of my mouth as I watched the trio stalk in our direction. 'Hey, there. What's up?'

'Whaddya mean, "what's up"?' Andy's arms crossed his chest in a parody of his uncle's, his eyes narrowed suspiciously. 'I thought you said that we were wanted by the police.'

'Wanted by the police? Are you? Have you told them that yet?' The innocent look on my face could have rivaled Bambi's. 'Miss Lucinda, did you know that Andy was wanted by the police when you hired him?'

By this time, Andy was sputtering, he was so mad. How in the world had I thought him good-looking, even for a second, I wondered, as I took in his flaring nostrils and the blotchy redness that now colored his face.

'You know good and well what I mean, you – you – you out-of-stater! Don't go putting words in my mouth! Uncle Joe, just what did she tell you?' He swung around to face his uncle.

Skinny Joe shrugged, the movement causing a ripple to cross his flabby chest. 'She said you were wanted out front. I told you, you came out here. End of story.'

The ruckus was causing us some unwanted attention. Two of the officers who were standing along the room's perimeter began to move in our direction.

'Oh, great, just what we needed: another visit from the fuzz,' I murmured to no one in particular. Miss Lucinda gave me an odd glance, but kept her own counsel.

Two of Manchester's finest approached our little group,

their faces set on 'bland' as they looked us over. Finally, the shorter officer, the one whose eyebrows were as thick as newly hatched caterpillars in the spring, turned to Miss Lucinda.

'Ma'am, are these young men bothering you?' Now that was a question I hadn't expected to hear. I camouflaged a small laugh behind a cough.

'No, Officer, they're not. Actually, they are friends of the – of the deceased. You might want to ask them a few questions about this evening, if you haven't done so already.' Miss Lucinda continued ministering to Miss Bea's shoulders.

'Is this true?' The taller of the pair, the one with the pale blue eyes and hair like cotton wool, looked at Andy and Bert with an interested look on his face.

'Well, yes, it is,' admitted Andy. Bert just stood there.

I've often heard the expression, "like a bump on a log," but it had never really occurred to me exactly what that meant. After observing Bert's behavior, though, I think I figured it out: bumps on a log don't move, that's true, but they also don t go away. If Andy had a hand in this, then so did Bert. The two were joined at the hip.

Chapter Twelve

I had apparently struck a nerve of Andy's with my glib twisting of his words. What was in his background that he didn't want known? Well, I'd leave the Manchester PD to worry about that one; I had Miss Lucinda and Miss Bea to deal with.

The two officers invited Andy to join them for a chat, and I watched as Bert began drifting in that direction as well. Two for the price of one, I thought, as a chair was pulled out for him as well. Andy wasn't happy about it; the daggers he was shooting in Bert's direction were as murderous as any I had ever seen.

'Jo?' I dragged my eyes from the boys back to Leslie, whose hand was tugging at my sleeve. 'Shouldn't one of us go and check on Lily? Maybe make sure that she's all right?'

Good grief. I had forgotten all about the girl. 'I'll go,' I said, thrusting my chair back from the table. I was beginning to feel like a glorified babysitter.

I sped across the dining area to the hallway. The door to the women's dressing room was open; I paused – had we left it that way? I couldn't be sure, but I had a feeling that one of us had closed it behind us. Oh, well; Lily is a big girl, I thought. (Of course, I meant as in 'grown up', not 'big' in build!)

The 'big girl' wasn't in the dressing room. Or the

bathroom. Or anywhere else that I hastily checked, a sense of panic rising in my throat. At least, I hoped that it was panic and not my last meal making its way back to the surface. This evening was not only going downhill, it was going subterranean. And fast.

As my mother is wont to say, 'It's going to hell in a handbasket.' I couldn't have said it better.

OK, I said to myself, think, Jo. Where else might she have gone? Home, maybe? That would entail a jaunt to her car, which was in the parking lot … the parking lot! Oh, no, I groaned inwardly. She'd see Josie and no one would be with her.

I darted down the hall, my long skirts caught up in my hands. It occurred to me then that I had been doing a lot of dashing about in these high-heeled shoes, and they weren't half bad. Maybe the women of the Old West did know a thing or two about comfort after all.

My mind was digressing, a sure sign that I was losing it. Hold it together, Jo, I admonished myself. First things first: report back to the Becklaw gals and tell them that Lily is nowhere to be found. They'll know what to do.

Why in the world had I thought that they would be any better at this than I was? As soon as I delivered my news, Miss Bea's face turned ashen, Miss Lucinda's mouth fell open and stayed that way, and Leslie's eyes filled with tears.

'What?' I demanded. I looked at each of them in turn, waiting for someone to enlighten me.

'Oh, Jo,' began Leslie, voice quavering. 'If someone is hunting down women and Lily's missing, she might be in danger, too! Poor Josie. Poor Lily.' She put her face into her hands.

Really, now. It's a wonder more people don't get hurt leaping to conclusions as quickly as they do, present party not included. My leaps of logic were based on – well, logic. I all but snapped my fingers in their faces to bring them back to reality.

'Look, just because I can't find her doesn't mean she's not here somewhere. I'm going back out to the parking lot and making sure she's not there. Or *is* there, as the case may be. Leslie?' I quirked an eyebrow at her in an invitation to join me.

'Miss Lucinda, will you two be OK?' Leslie stood to her feet, hesitating briefly. I absolutely adored such displays of loyalty. We were becoming a very tight-knit group indeed.

'We'll be fine, my dear,' said Miss Lucinda bravely. I noticed she had included Miss Bea in her answer, although she might have begun speaking in terms of the royal 'we'. Either way, I was sure the two of them would be perfectly all right.

Leslie and I wove our way through the scattered tables and back out the front door. An evening chill had settled in earnest now, and I wished that I'd grabbed my jacket while I was in the dressing room. I shivered. It occurred to me the shiver might not be only from the coolness in the air.

We paused at the edge of the parking lot, each scanning the scene for a glimpse of Lily's bright pink costume. Of course, she might have tossed a sweater or something on top of it; the more I thought about that, the more likely it seemed. Lily was as modest as they came.

'Let's walk over and ask that officer whether or not anyone has seen Lily out here.' I said to Leslie, pointing out the young woman in a Manchester uniform. 'She might not even be here, you know.' I put action to my words and began striding toward the policewoman, Leslie hurrying to catch up.

'I hope you're right, Jo,' Leslie said. 'I'd really hate for her to see ...' – she gulped – 'for her to see Josie this way without anyone with her.'

Leslie was so tenderhearted sometimes; it was no wonder that LJ felt safe with her.

'I agree,' I replied, 'which is why I'm going to ask this nice officer,' I paused, looking at the shiny badge on the woman's uniform jacket, 'this nice Officer Kingsley if she might have seen our friend Lily.' I smiled in what I hoped was a friendly fashion at the poker-faced officer. My lips felt like they were stuck against my teeth, my mouth had gone so dry.

'Who are you looking for?' The question was directed at me, although I caught the swift glance that took in Leslie as well. Boy, these officers had quick eyes. They probably saw everything and then some.

'We are part of Becklaw's Murder Mystery Tour – not a real murder, I mean – and the, er … deceased is, or was, a part of our play.' Great, Jo. You sure knew how to fumble the verbal ball. I must have sounded halfway sensible to Officer Kingsley, though. She extracted a notepad from the breast pocket of her jacket and unclipped the pen that came with it.

'OK, first things first. Name?' She waited, pen poised over the pad. I stared at her a bit dumbly. Name? What name? My name?

She must have been able to read thoughts because she smiled kindly at me. 'I need the name of the person you're trying to find, ma'am.'

Oh. That name. 'Lily.' There. I felt as triumphant as if I had produced the Golden Ticket.

'Last name?' Again the pen was ready to write.

I turned to look at Leslie, who in turn shrugged helplessly. We hadn't even learned Lily's last name. Brilliant.

'I don't know,' I admitted, sounding to my ears like someone who wasn't too sure of anything. 'You could try looking for her dress, though.' Great, Jo. That sounded even more stupid, if such a thing were possible at that moment.

'Her dress?' I'll say this for Officer Kingsley: she was one cool cat, not even batting an eye when I made my goofy suggestion.

Leslie hurried to speak, apparently not trusting me to produce a coherent description of what Lily had been wearing the last time we saw her. That made sense, though, I had to admit. Leslie *had* dressed the girl.

As Leslie gave Officer Kingsley the pertinent information, I turned to look around the parking lot again, hoping to spot Lily. Instead, the person I did see caused me to drop my jaw, much as Miss Lucinda had just minutes ago.

Standing as close as he could to the taped-off area stood Skinny Joe. He seemed to be alternately looking at Josie – who was now covered, thank goodness and may God rest her soul – or peering at the ground. What was this man's game? I wondered. A tug at my sleeve drew my attention.

'Jo? Officer Kingsley said that when they find her,'– her tone had stressed the 'when' – 'she or someone else will let us know. In the meantime, we need to get back inside with Miss Bea and Miss Lucinda.'

'Sounds good,' I answered. My voice must have had an inflection in it because both the cop and Leslie stared at me. I smiled at the two of them, giving them my best Cheshire Cat impression.

'All righty then,' Leslie commented to no one in particular. 'And thanks, Officer. We'll wait to hear something from you.' With her hand clinging firmly to my arm, she began marching us across the parking lot and up the walkway that led to the dining room.

A few feet from the door, she stopped abruptly,

spinning me around to face her. 'OK, Jo. What gives? I know that tone you used back there. Something's up.' She stood there, arms crossed and eyes boring into mine.

'I saw ...' I hesitated, trying to work out what it was that I had seen.

'You saw what, Jo?' Leslie could be impatient when she wanted, which was now, apparently.

I took in a deep breath and made up my mind. 'I saw Skinny Joe out there by Josie, staring at her and looking around on the ground like he'd lost something.' There. I'd given voice to my thoughts. I waited while Leslie digested my words.

She narrowed her eyes. 'Are you saying that Joe might have killed her?'

'No. Yes. Oh, I don't know, Leslie!' I sounded snappish, but I was getting mighty tired of folks thinking that I always had the answers. 'Well, maybe.'

'Hmm.' She hadn't noticed my tone, thank goodness. 'Let's say he did it. What would he have been looking for?'

I thought for a moment. 'Maybe he dropped something? Something that could be tied directly to him?'

'OK,' nodded Leslie. 'That makes sense. Let's go with that. What might he have dropped?'

Out of the corner of my left eye, I could see a bulky figure moving our way. Actually, moving directly toward us. And fairly fast, which was amazing, considering that it was not-so-Skinny Joe.

'Ah, Leslie, let's take this inside,' I suggested, taking my turn at sleeve-grabbing and trying to move us into the veritable safety of the dining room.

Too late. In the few seconds it took Leslie to register what I said, then turn and get an eyeful of the heft closing in on us, we were trapped. Joe stood between us and the door, effectively blocking our chance at escape.

Just then, I felt like that wriggling mouse Derek had caught on that first morning at Miss Bea's: I had nowhere to run except in circles.

He said nothing, but instead stood there with his beefy hands on his hips, nostrils flared in anger and eyes fairly snapping sparks.

What is it about the vacuum of silence that we humans deem it necessary to fill it?

I filled it, all right.

The gibberish that came from my mouth had a funny effect on Skinny Joe. His hands dropped to his sides, his eyes opened to their widest, and he took a step back from me as if to protect himself from the nonsense spilling from my lips. Although I can't recall my exact words, here is a paraphrased version:

'I saw you, Joe. I saw you looking around on the ground for whatever it was that you dropped when you brutally murdered that poor Josie. In fact, I've already reported my suspicions to the police. If I were you, I'd run.'

Or something to that effect. Leslie told me later that I not only accused him of Josie's death, but also global warming, the rise in gasoline prices, and the disappearance of Jimmy Hoffa. While I don't recall that, I can say I certainly lit a fire under that man's massive behind. He was off like a shot.

Chapter Thirteen

The rest of the evening passed by in a blur. We each had our turn with the officers and were finally cleared to leave. Miss Bea then did a most surprising thing: she let Derek drive.

I sat in the front seat with him and Miss Lucinda, squeezed between them like an almost empty tube of toothpaste. Leslie and Miss Bea sat on either side of LJ in the back, Miss Bea leaning close to LJ's huge arm for comfort. Or because she was afraid of falling out of the car. LJ did take up quite a bit of real estate.

The drive to the KOA site was depressingly quiet. I couldn't think of a single clever comment to make, and even Derek's dry humor seemed to be in hiding. A pall had fallen over us – I've always wanted to use that phrase – and settled in around our group like a thick blanket. Even though none of us knew Josie that well, her untimely death was firmly connected with Becklaw's Murder Mystery Tour, and Becklaw's Murder Mystery Tour was firmly connected with the six of us.

Lily still had not shown her face. A 'Possible Missing Person' report was taken by Officer Kingsley, who assured us that Lily had probably been spooked by the entire episode. On the other hand, we still hadn't been able to reach her on her cell. It was a worrisome issue, that was for sure.

Derek piloted the station wagon smoothly down the highway and to the KOA, pulling into the wide driveway just as the dashboard clock showed eleven o'clock. Maybe it was because of the fact that I saw the time, but suddenly I was dead on my feet. Oops, I corrected myself. A better turn of phrase might be in order.

We paused in front of Miss Lucinda's trailer, and I walked with her to the door to make sure that she made it in safely. Actually, I had an ulterior motive. As we reached the top step leading to her door, I whispered *sotto voce*, 'Where do you think that Lily is? Do you reckon something happened to her as well?'

I truly was worried about her. Somehow I just couldn't picture her being so perturbed that she would leave the fairgrounds without telling anyone where she was going.

Miss Lucinda, bless her heart, did not miss a beat, using the moment she unlocked the door to whisper back, 'I think she's in on it.'

And in she walked, leaving me on the steps with my mouth hanging wide open. I seemed to be doing that a lot lately. My mother would warn me about catching flies.

Next stop was our trailer. Derek had agreed to take charge of checking it out for us after parking the car, then walk with LJ back to their abode, and that suited me and the other gals just fine. I was jumpy and all I needed was going into a dark trailer with two other women who were as nervous as I was.

LJ and Derek made a quick sweep of the trailer's interior, assuring us that no one had come in since we had left earlier that evening. With that reassurance, we felt safe enough to dash up the steps, slam the door behind us, and quickly throw the two locks. I could swear I heard Derek chuckling as he and LJ began their short walk back toward the front of the campground.

Miss Bea perched on the edge of the couch, an unhappy

look on her face. She was feeling responsible for this entire escapade, I could tell, and I moved over to put a comforting arm around her. Leslie had the same thought, and the three of us huddled together on the sofa, arms entwined and silent as church mice. Neither one of us could think of a single consoling word to help Miss Bea feel better.

At least no one could accuse us of being a pair of Job's Comforters.

Finally Miss Bea stirred herself, shook off our arms, and stood to her feet. 'I'll make us some tea,' she said miserably. Sweet Miss Bea – always taking care of others and yet not knowing how to take care of herself. Off she tottered to the kitchen, a little black rain cloud almost visible over her head.

The tea was hot, strong, and sweet. Leslie had followed Miss Bea into the kitchen and thoughtfully added some fudge-filled sandwich cookies to the tray, so we were definitely working our way toward a sugar overload. Oh, well: I'd always heard that sugary tea helps to calm overwrought nerves. Of course, if that were true, Great Britain should be jitter-free. I'm not too sure that I was convinced. But I was willing to give it a try. I don't know if I felt calm or just hung over on sugar by the time I got to bed, but whichever was the case, I fell asleep as soon as my weary head hit the pillow.

I'm not certain what woke me. At first I wasn't even sure if I was awake or having a very real dream, the kind of dream that stays with you for days after. Somewhere in the distance I could hear a high tinkling sound, something like the sound that Tinker Bell might make. (I know – silly comparison. But I can't think of anything else, and Tinker Bell does tinkle. So there.) Whatever it was, I thought it was lovely.

I lay there a fraction longer, another noise edging out

the crystalline echo. It was much louder, and by then I figured out that I was not asleep at all. My heart was well ahead of my brain at the moment, and had already detached itself from my chest and had leapfrogged into my throat. A series of thuds seemed to be coming from the front room, and I thought I could also detect the sound of feet shushing over the carpet.

Moving as carefully as I could, I eased the covers back from my neck and shoulders where I had bunched them up around me for security the night before. It's amazing just how loud sheets can sound when you're trying to move quietly.

I managed to extract myself from the bed and began to tiptoe over to the bedroom door, pausing to grab the hairbrush I had laid on the nightstand. I'm not too sure what I thought I could do with that, but I felt armed.

Now I could hear definite movement from the front of the trailer. I strained my ears to hear what was going on out there; I was trying to see if there was more than one person, but the level of noise told me that it was probably just one person.

Just one person? I mentally scolded myself. *One* burglar in the place was one too many. I tried to hear movement from Leslie's or Miss Bea's rooms, but the soft duet of snores told me that they were out dead to the world.

Oh, good grief, Jo, I thought to myself. You are really going to have to clean up your vocabulary. Let me rephrase that: Miss Bea and Leslie were out cold. Not what I meant to say, but you get the drift.

The defense of our happy little home was apparently up to me, so I quickly hatched a plan. I would leap out of my room, brandish my hairbrush in the burglar's startled – and hopefully scared – face and scream like a banshee. I could do it, too. When my brothers would tease me, I could send up a screech that would make any fire siren proud. I figured that my scream would act as an alarm for Miss Bea and Leslie, and, if the truth be told, probably most of the KOA visitors as well.

Taking a deep breath, I wrenched open my door, took a running leap out of my room, and let off a scream that could have woken the dead. Oops – wrong sentiment. But you get the idea.

I'm not sure who was the more startled: me or Lily.

Doors began banging open as Miss Bea and Leslie stumbled from their respective rooms, looks of pure terror on their faces. I had stayed frozen in place, my mouth still wide open and my eyes following suit. Lily looked like a participant in the childhood game of 'Statues', one hand hovering over Miss Bea's large handbag and one holding a piece of paper aloft.

Did I mention doors banging open? Yes, I managed to awaken at least three neighbors on each side of us, most of whom came charging toward our trailer in various stages of dress, or undress, as the case may be. It took a while to calm everyone down enough to leave and return to their own trailers, but Miss Bea, bless her heart, managed to do it. I could tell our KOA buddies were now positive a basket case was vacationing next to them.

I wanted to say: Huh. You haven't met Crazy Great-Aunt Opal.

Back to Lily. As I mentioned, I caught her red-handed, digging through Miss Bea's capacious handbag in the darkness of our trailer's front room. By the time that we had shooed the neighbors back to their respective beds and had turned our attention to Lily, she had moved from the 'scared spitless' stage to one of defiance. That, to me, was odd, considering she was somewhere she wasn't supposed to be and was still considered a missing person. Lily, though, seemed to feel that we owed her the explanation of why I had not only frightened her but also come bouncing at her with a hairbrush.

Sometimes the world spins around on its axis, and sometimes the universe seems to turn on its head. This was definitely a head-over-heels moment.

Chapter Fourteen

Lily sat on the sofa, hands clasped in her lap and her feet set primly together on the floor. If I hadn't known better, I would have thought that this year's must-have color was black when it came to clothing styles; Lily's black pants, black turtleneck and black tennis shoes were either cutting-edge stylish or she was emulating a cat burglar.

My vote was on the latter.

Leslie, Miss Bea, and I stood in a row in front of the sofa and its occupant, as sober as judges and waiting to see who would blink first, so to speak. Lily blinked.

'I know I shouldn't have just let myself in like I did,' – huge eye roll from me and Leslie, especially since the glass from the broken window was *clearly* sparkling on the floor – 'but I really needed to find out what happened to Josie.' She stopped, assumed a pious expression, and waited for a response.

Boy, did I ever have a response for her. However, Miss Bea saved me from further embarrassing myself by jumping into the conversational void.

'I'm not sure what you thought you'd find in my handbag,' Miss Bea said, giving a significant look at the purse that was now well out of Lily's reach. 'I have no more idea about what took place tonight than you do.'

I wanted so badly to add, 'Or do you know more than

you're letting on?' That, I think, might have been a trifle too much at this point. Be that as it may, Miss Bea's words still caused Lily to flush angrily and become defensive. What was the world coming to when a burglar blamed the burglaree for causing the break-in?

'If someone had been so kind as to explain to me what was going on tonight, I wouldn't have had to do this. I happen to be the librarian of Manchester Public Library, and I'll have you know that my character is without blemish,' Lily huffed, folding her scrawny arms across an equally scrawny chest. (No wonder she wanted that 'modesty panel' in her costume, I thought.)

Oh, ho! Here was leverage worth using, I thought, with a somewhat malicious grin. There was no way on God's green earth that someone like Lily would want their precious reputation tarnished with something as vile as breaking and entering.

'If you'll beg my pardon for interrupting, Miss Bea, I'd like to know exactly what it was that Lily thought she might find here. At night. In our trailer.'

My words were directed at Miss Bea but my eyes were on Lily. My, she was one cool customer. Without breaking a sweat, Lily managed to exude 'hurt feelings' and 'I can't believe you'd even ask that', all with just a sigh and a full-blown eye roll.

Leslie spoke up, and the rest of us stared at her. What she had to say made sense when I didn't think that common sense could enter this convoluted equation.

'Miss Bea, I think that we should be asking Lily where she was for those hours immediately following the discovery of the ...' She hesitated, still having an issue with the word 'body'. 'With finding Josie, I mean.'

She returned Lily's stare with one of her own. I might actually place Leslie's 'stare' in the 'glare' department. I was so proud of her I could burst, but I satisfied myself with an 'atta girl' and an air-five, Miss Bea's bulk separating us from an actual hand slap.

'For your information, Miss Nosey, I had to run back to my apartment for something. When I got back to the fairground, there was a roadblock, so I just turned around and went back home.' Lily's nose elevated itself in the air.

I had to laugh. 'Miss Nosey'? Coming from Lily-who-broke-into-our-place-and-rifled-Miss-Bea's-handbag?

That was certainly rich, I thought wryly.

Miss Bea, bless her sweet soul, quickly put a stop to the sniping before it got going in earnest. She turned to Leslie and asked her to put the tea kettle on. 'Oh, and bring out the rest of the cookies, won't you, dear?' Leslie nodded and headed for the kitchen, but I stubbornly stayed put; I wasn't about to miss anything.

I figured if I didn't meet Miss Bea's eyes, I wouldn't feel the need to join Leslie. Keeping my gaze carefully on Lily and watching Miss Bea with my awesome peripheral vision, I clamped my mouth shut and took a seat next to Lily, who promptly scooted to the end of the sofa. Talk about childish! I could see Miss Bea eyeing me for a moment, but she turned her attention back on Lily with a small sigh.

Sorry, Miss Bea. I was disappointing her, I was sure, but the need to know was greater than the need to obey.

As I've mentioned before, we humans have an innate need to fill silence with noise. Miss Bea, apparently well acquainted with this particular foible, sat and waited patiently for Lily to begin talking. Although I was itching to say something, I followed the lead of my employer and sat with my hands folded in my lap. It was a strategy that soon paid dividends. Unfortunately, at the time we didn't realize it, but hindsight is a vision-cleanser.

Clearing her throat a bit nervously, Lily began talking. 'I was sitting in the dressing room, waiting for someone to come and get me, when I realized that I'd left my cellphone at home. I really need to keep it with me at all times, especially since my mother has been so ill. Anyway, I decided I had enough time before the performance to get there and back, so I took off. I'd parked in the side lot. You know, the one that some of the food vendors use? There was an empty spot there, so I figured, why not? I mean, we all have the same kind of parking placard.

'Like I already said, I ran to my apartment, grabbed my cell, and got back as soon as I could. Only, when I got here, the police weren't letting any cars through, so I had to turn around and go home. I heard about the murder on the news, so I decided to come over and see what you all knew. No one answered the door, though, and I just knew that you'd understand if I let myself in.' Here Lily paused for breath, looking from me to Miss Bea, trying to read our faces.

First of all, I was amazed that she could justify her trespassing as 'letting herself in'. Now that would make for an interesting police report, I mused. Next, I felt as though something in her tale sounded off, but I couldn't put my finger on it just then. Finally, it blew me away that Lily could even entertain the idea that Miss Bea was that naïve.

Oh, how wrong I was.

Miss Bea's kindness was never more evident than at that moment, but as I mentioned before, this was all hindsight. Over tea and the rest of our cookie stash, the four of us managed to have a fairly decent conversation, moving from poor Josie to life as a librarian to the future of our troupe. Finally Lily patted her lips with a napkin and stood to leave, smiling at the three of us. I alone noticed that the smile did not reach her eyes. Leslie and Miss Bea tend to believe in the good of people. I, thankfully, am not afflicted with that inconvenient virtue.

I pulled out the vacuum that was kept in the trailer's pantry and attempted to clean up the glass shards that still littered the carpet like pieces of a falling star. Leslie carried the tea things to the kitchen; I could hear her and Miss Bea chatting amiably as they washed up and put away the teacups. I was dead beat and the idea of holding a friendly conversation at that time of night – correction, that time of morning – was not my cup of tea.

Oops. My humor must've been tired as well. Please pardon the pun, dear reader.

We finally retired to our respective rooms, and I found myself turning the lock on the bedroom door, something I would not have done before the Lily incident. I could hear Leslie and Miss Bea doing the same, so at least I was reassured that I was not being paranoid. On the other hand, if I *was* paranoid, then so were they. Not that this comforted me much, but there you have it.

I did get a few hours of shut-eye, but not the deep sleep needed for true rest. I staggered from the bed at ten o'clock, yawning and stretching and attempting to coax myself into feeling like facing the day.

Leslie was still in bed, but Miss Bea already sat at the breakfast table, looking as pert and perky as a robin. In fact, she brought to mind one cheeky little fellow I had spotted in the parking lot of Skinny Joe's Steakhouse and Brewery. He – or she, perhaps, not being a bird expert – had sat watching me as I walked by, not even flinching when my cellphone had trilled out 'Ode to Joy' as I passed. Miss Bea was just like that, I thought. She didn't flinch or scare easily, but instead contented herself with letting what would be happen without bouncing up and down the emotional scale.

The bird analogy stuck with me as we moved through that day. I began to notice, really notice, some of her mannerisms: the slight tilt of the head when listening to someone speak, the bright eyes that darted around the room, and the tiny bites as she daintily consumed her meals. Goodness, I thought. I had never been around so many examples of wildlife! Even the people in my life seemed to be more creature-like than I was used to.

I wonder if this was how Crazy Great-Aunt Opal got her start toward the Wonderful Land of Make-Believe.

Chapter Fifteen

The performances, of course, were all cancelled, of necessity. The fair organizers still offered us two-thirds of our fee, thankfully, so at least we didn't lose much in that department. I guess we could have packed up and hightailed it back to Copper and the lodge, but Miss Bea thought we should remain where we were, at least until the police had concluded their investigation. In reality, I was glad to stay. It would have driven me clean over the edge of sanity to leave without knowing what was up.

And I guess I felt some slim margin of responsibility toward Josie. The poor girl was only signing on to portray a victim of murder, not really be one.

Something was moving around in my mind, trying to find the passage that would lead from the subconscious to the active brain, but I still couldn't quite pin down what it was. I let it go for the present; there were still quite a few other issues to focus on rather than stew over an idea that may or may not play a role in the investigation.

One of the aforementioned issues was that of Andy and Bert. 'Angry' doesn't even begin to describe how they were feeling. What with the police interviews (they had a total of three, if you can believe that), the loss of a part-time job (not our fault) and the fact that they had been told not to leave the area (which included heading off to the casino where they both worked), those two were emotional wrecks.

Skinny Joe was another problem. He continued to skulk around the fairgrounds, looking for heaven-knew-what and giving the investigators a hard time, accusing them of wasting valuable taxpayers' monies with the harassment of his nephew (his words, not mine). On top of that, he had the nerve to come looking for Miss Bea the very day following Josie's demise, but we four ran defense for her and effectively ran him out of Dodge.

Percy and Oleta McLaughlin were also an issue, but not as bad as they might have been. If that had been the case, I would have very firmly insisted to Miss Bea that we were leaving. That instant. The McLaughlins were the typical bystanders at an accident: not really wanting to stare but unable to contain themselves. When the pair of them arrived next afternoon with a plate of home-made muffins and an eager look on their faces, I could do nothing but allow them in to pry and ask question after question.

They were somewhat of a help, though. Percy had replaced the window right away, and Oleta, bless her gossipy heart, could hardly wait to share with us what she'd heard about Josie from her sister, who had gotten it from her daughter, a cashier at the supermarket, who had gone to school with Josie.

Miss Josie, to no one's surprise, had not been the model of virtue during her high school career. A brief fling in her sophomore year with a professor ended her college endeavor, and the most recent bit of information had her linked with a married bank teller. Whether this were true or not, I still felt mighty uncomfortable discussing the newly departed's life so callously. I had to get away from it, so I offered to make tea to go with the muffins, which, by the way, were cranberry orange, one of my favorites.

Leslie was upset by the talk as well. That was obvious to me the second she walked into the kitchen, mere steps behind me. Leslie prefers to see the best in others, and listening to someone being verbally masticated did not jive with her credo of 'live and let live'.

There were some days that I felt I was surrounded by saints. Thank goodness for Miss Lucinda.

Speaking of whom, Miss Lucinda had given up the rental of her small trailer and moved in with us. I was a bit uneasy when she made the suggestion, but was instantly put at my ease when she announced that she would share 'her dear Beatrice's room', something that 'dear Beatrice' did not seem too crazy about. But Miss Bea, being Miss Bea, displayed a stiff upper lip to go with the moustache that she was sporting (apparently the woman waxed, and simply hadn't had the time or inclination to do so recently) and said nothing.

With our party now complete, we four women held a powwow on the second day following the murder, trying to determine the best course of action to take. I suppose we had all somehow decided to take on the mystery ourselves, not trusting the professionals to do it correctly.

Leslie was all for following Lily around town, hoping to catch her public confession that yes, she had murdered Josie in a fit of rage. Or pique. Or whatever type of fit it is that killers have. With no evidence that pointed to Lily as the killer, though, we finally had to drop that idea.

I personally had my money on Skinny Joe. Well, actually, I thought it might have been Skinny Joe *and* Andy working together but, again, the motive angle was a bit fuzzy.

Miss Bea felt that the Andy angle – Andy solo, not in a duet – might be the more obvious line of inquiry. That was filed under 'perhaps' for us to take a look at later.

Miss Lucinda was silent, her eyes closed and her lips moving in silent conversation with herself. Or with her evil familiars. That in fact would not surprise me. With that wild lavender hair and the malevolent grin she trotted out from time to time, Miss Lucinda reminded me of the wacky witch Madame Mim in *The Sword in the Stone*. (Remember? The one who challenges Merlin and becomes all sorts of crazy-looking creatures?)

When she finally opened her eyes and spoke, it could have been Mandarin Chinese for all the sense she made.

'Still waters run deep,' Miss Lucinda announced, looking solemnly at the three of us, who stared back in confusion. Being around this woman sure took care of my homesickness; she was the *doppelgänger* for you-know-who, residing back in Piney Woods, enjoying the 'luxury lifestyle' at her assisted-living apartments.

Leslie was the first to respond. Choosing her words carefully, modulating her tone as if dealing with a child, she asked, 'Could you please explain what it is you mean, Miss Lucinda?'

Miss Lucinda snorted. 'I certainly can explain. Now you listen to me, the three of you. Who is the one person who had the means and possibly the motive and has not been questioned even once by the police, at least that we know of?' She gave us all the Mrs Fiornelli fish-eye, waiting for one of us to raise our hand and give the correct answer.

I did. Believe you me, it was an automatic response. There is something about a teacher – or someone who can channel 'teacher'– that instantly throws me into student mode.

'Yes, Jo?' Good grief, I thought, I feel like I'm sitting back in Stonewall Jackson Elementary, trying to earn brownie points with Mrs Fiornelli.

'I think,' I began hesitantly, 'that you are speaking of Julian Sweet.'

I didn't need to hear her response; the triumphant look on her face confirmed it.

Now it was Miss Bea's turn to snort. These Becklaw Women are eloquent snorters, I'd discovered.

'Lucinda Becklaw, as usual, you have come to one of the most ignorant conclusions that not even the Easter Bunny would believe in.' Wait a minute, I thought, what did the good ol' EB have to do with this? There had better be some 'Splainin, Lucy. Well, not Lucy, *per se*, but you get the Desi drift.

The look of disdain that Miss Lucinda shot at Miss Bea was troubling. After all, these two gals were sharing a bedroom. I really didn't want another murder on our hands.

'First of all,' she said, giving Miss Bea a hard stare before turning to me and Leslie, 'Julian wasn't in the dressing room when you went to see what that Skinny Joe creature was up to, remember?'

'We don't know that,' Leslie protested. 'We only saw Joe standing at the dressing room door and heard him call for Andy and Bert. For all we know, Julian could have been in there as well and just busy.'

Miss Lucinda nodded her head in acknowledgement. 'I considered that, Leslie. But this is why I don't think he was there at all: the officers swept the dining hall and all of the rooms, including dressing rooms, and no one else *was* in there. I think that when we were all focused on getting our costumes on, he must have slipped out to wait for Josie for some reason known only to him, confronted her about something, got angry, and killed her.'

We three in the audience sat silently, letting Miss Lucinda's words roll around in our heads. It did make sense in an odd way, I thought. We'd been concentrating on the people we saw, rather than the ones we didn't see. And Julian definitely fit the latter category.

'Could it be possible,' I began, 'that Julian had gone back out to his car? Maybe totally missed seeing Josie?'

'Hmm. Maybe,' answered Miss Lucinda thoughtfully. 'I think I would have seen him out there, though. Remember, I had to go back out to get something that Derek had left in the station wagon. I think the very fact that I didn't see him points to his involvement somehow.'

Now that was convoluted reasoning! Crazy Great-Aunt Opal ... well, you know. She'd probably pound Miss Lucinda on the back and welcome her to the Nutter's Club if she could have heard us talking just then.

'OK,' I replied. 'Let me get this straight: you didn't see Julian out in the parking lot and he wasn't in the building, so he must be the killer.'

'Precisely.' Miss Lucinda beamed at me as if I had won the spelling bee. Oh, boy. This was beginning to make sense to me, and I didn't even know what I was talking about.

Miss Bea rose to her feet a bit stiffly, clutching the edge of the table for support.

'I suggest we adjourn and have some sustenance, girls. No one can think on an empty stomach. "Empty stomach, empty mind", as my beloved Desmond would always say.'

I think I felt the oncoming shock waves of Miss Lucinda's response before she even opened her mouth. Leslie must have as well, because she seemed to shrink back a bit and edge toward Miss Bea.

'Your Desmond must have been one smart cookie then, Beatrice. The last time I saw him, his girth was as large as a man twice his height.' With that salvo, Miss Lucinda rose to her feet as well, the two of them glaring at each other from the opposite sides of the table.

Well. This little exchange was getting us nowhere but fast. I decided to take charge.

'Miss Bea, Miss Lucinda. With all due respect, the enemy is Out There, not In Here. If the two of you could remain civil just long enough for us to finish this conversation, I think we might latch on to something worth pursuing.'

Aha. I'd done it now, I thought in a brief moment of panic. The Becklaw Barrage turned toward me as if one brain in two bodies, their combined glares laser-like in intensity.

Leslie's face mirrored the shock I was feeling, and she had that little 'mouse running in a circle' look in her eyes. But, brave woman that she was, she attempted to defuse the situation.

'Ah, Jo, that is … er … a great idea. I mean, if Miss Bea and Miss Lucinda think so, that is.' With that little gem hanging in space, some of the passion melted from the Becklaw visages. I silently applauded Leslie, who was now glistening with nervous sweat. Miss Bea came to her senses first, turning to Leslie with her patented gentle smile.

'I'm so sorry, Leslie. I get a bit 'het up' about things like this, and then it always seems to get out of hand, doesn't it?' That, I think, seemed to be directed at her sister-in-law.

Miss Lucinda apparently agreed with me. Her face shifted from fiery intensity to glacial freeze, but to her credit, she kept her mouth clamped shut.

I think that was a true 'defining moment' for the four of us gals. In spite of the fireworks, we began to work together in earnest, and the end result was nothing short of miraculous. Without knowing it at that moment, we had solved the murder of Josie, 'lady of the night'.

Chapter Sixteen

Next day we decided to drive back into town, the six of us, and see what the Manchester Police Department was up to. Actually, we were going to check and see if anyone had been arrested, confessed, or otherwise helped to conclude this entire affair.

Officer Kingsley, that nice policewoman (policeperson?) from the crime scene, was on duty and available to take our questions. She found a room large enough to accommodate us all and took us back *en masse,* an impromptu parade of amateur sleuths determined to be involved. I confess that I did some minor snooping as we walked through the halls, hoping to catch a glimpse of detectives at work or in conference. I'm not too sure what I thought I'd learn from this little exercise, but who knew? Detecting might be transferable via osmosis.

Officer K located the empty conference room and led us inside, flipping on lights and pulling out chairs for us all. That surprised me, I think. For some reason, I always thought that police officers didn't turn their backs on others. Or maybe that was only on police shows. Anyway, we all took a seat and she sat looking at us expectantly, waiting to hear what we had to say.

I could see that, once again, I would need to take the lead on this one, so I cleared my throat, looked straight at Officer Kingsley, and launched into the theories we had defined and discussed the night before. Once I began speaking, I realized why the others were hesitant to open their mouths: I sounded, well, a little off-balance.

'We were talking,' I indicated Miss Bea, Miss Lucinda and Leslie, 'and may have come up with some possible suspects for you.' I waited for Officer Kingsley to reply, perhaps with an enthusiastic, 'Oh, I knew you could do it!' or something to that effect.

The look she gave me, though, was anything but encouraging. It was then I realized most detectives don't like being told that someone else has detected for them, especially if it is a lay person such as me and my fellow troupers. 'Oh?' That one word, accompanied with an eyebrow lift, spoke volumes. Thankfully, the other theorists in the room decided to join in.

Miss Bea gave me a quick glance that said 'Be quiet for a minute', and I telegraphed one back that said, 'No prob … you go for it.' She turned toward Officer Kingsley and began laying out our ideas, beginning with who we suspected and why we had, or had not, eliminated them. Officer K, to her credit, listened politely. That is, until we got to Julian Sweet.

'I could not find him anywhere, and when the gals went to collect Andy from the men's dressing room, the only others there were Bert and Skinny Joe, Andy's uncle.'

Miss Bea turned to Miss Lucinda, and she took up the story.

'And I didn't see him when I went out to the parking lot to get something that Derek had left behind in the station wagon,' Miss Lucinda added, nodding for emphasis. This movement sent her hair sliding, and a hunk of it hung low over one eyebrow, giving her a lop-sided look.

'Wait.' Officer Kingsley's hands lifted 'halt mode' as if directing traffic. 'Are you ladies saying that because you *didn't* see him there, you think he did it?' Her face was a blend of incredulity and interest. Something had piqued her curiosity.

'Well, yes, that's exactly what we're saying,' Miss Lucinda replied, looking at the rest of us to support her answer. We all vigorously nodded our heads like a herd of bobblehead dolls, even the boys. They had been filled in on our ideas on the way to the station.

'I see,' Officer K said slowly, and I think that she really *did* see what we were trying to get at because she pulled a notebook from her pocket and uncapped the pen attached to it. 'OK. Begin at the beginning. Tell me exactly why you suspect Julian Sweet. And don't leave out anything, even if you think it's insignificant.'

This was getting exciting, no doubt about it. I had never in my life had so many unique experiences, and I had to lay the credit at Neva's feet. Without her obsession with magazine subscriptions, I would still be back in Piney Woods, having to babysit the huge collection of Anderson nieces and nephews, and going stark raving mad.

Maybe that's what happened to Crazy Great-Aunt Opal. The Anderson clan has always had a ton of kids running around.

We unanimously allowed Miss Lucinda to take the lead on this, since she was the one whose brain came up with it to begin with. Her rendition went something like this:

'I had to go back out to the car because something we needed for the costumes had been left behind. Everyone was busy, so I just went without telling anyone. I'd already seen Andy and Bert arrive earlier, and overheard them saying that Julian had pulled in right behind them. And that Skinny Joe pranced by me as well, so I knew that all the menfolk were accounted for. When you're putting on a show,'– here Miss Bea managed to control an eye roll – 'you can't emphasize enough that timing is everything, and includes showing up when you're told to.'

'Anyway, I knew Josie was the only one not there yet, and thought I'd see if she was in her car, gabbing on the phone or to Julian, who still hadn't come inside. I walked over to the car, dropped my keys, and that's when ...'

Her voice faltered a bit, but who could blame the woman. She swallowed and continued.

'When I bent down to get the keys, I saw what I thought were feet on the other side of the car, only they were at an odd angle, not standing but instead, well, lying there and I ...' she swallowed again '... and I just knew that it was Josie. I don't know how I knew but I did.' Miss Lucinda completed her monologue and Officer Kingsley looked up for the notebook in which she had been furiously writing.

'Is there anything else, anything that might have something to do with this case? Did anyone see Josie when she arrived? Does anyone remember speaking to her? And can anyone beside Andy and Bert,' – she checked her notes – 'claim to have noticed Julian during this time?' Officer K looked around the table at each of us, waiting for more information. Finally Derek spoke up.

'Er, I think that I saw Julian walking in the direction of the parking lot, maybe around the time that Andy and Bert were coming in the door. I mean, I can't be sure, but I saw him later and he had on a dark blue sweatshirt and jeans, and the person I saw had those on as well. Of course, it was from a distance ...' Derek's voice petered out and he looked uncertainly from Officer Kingsley to Miss Lucinda.

'Wait,' I said suddenly. 'Didn't Andy have on the same thing? Or something pretty close?'

Derek thought for a moment, tilting his head in a good imitation of Miss Bea.

'Maybe,' he replied slowly.

130

'Come to think of it,' Leslie spoke up. 'didn't you have jeans and a sweatshirt yesterday as well, Jo?'

Six sets of eyes swiveled in my direction sudden suspicion causing at least a couple pairs to narrow slightly.

'Oh, come on, you guys,' I protested. 'Give me some credit here. Why would I want to do way with Josie? I didn't even know her before our trip to Manchester. Wouldn't it be more logical that someone who actually *knew* her did this? Or perhaps a random stranger? That makes more sense that saying I did it.' I crossed my arms across my chest, practically huffing and puffing in my indignation.

'Now, now, dear,' soothed Miss Bea. 'Leslie didn't say that you did anything. She was just pointing out that more than one person was dressed in the same fashion. Isn't that right, Leslie?' She turned toward Leslie for confirmation, whose face by this time was scarlet with embarrassment.

'Yes, that's what I meant, Miss Bea. And sorry, Jo. I wasn't trying to say that you killed Josie. That wasn't worded very well.' She gave me a hesitant smile.

I contemplated keeping the annoyance on my face, for a few minutes at least, but that's really not my style. I returned Leslie's smile and she relaxed visibly, settling back into her chair. It would take more than mere semantics to break us apart, I thought gratefully. Leslie was turning out to be a true friend.

'OK, folks. I think I've got enough to go on for now. But if any of you can think of something else, anything, give me a call.' Officer Kingsley stood to her feet and the rest of us did likewise. 'Here's my card. My cell number is there, as well as the office number. And you can text if you'd prefer.' She handed her cards around, and I tucked mine into my front jeans pocket.

It was close to lunchtime, and I proposed to Miss Bea and Miss Lucinda that we go eat. 'But let's go to Skinny

Joe's,' I suggested. 'That'll give us some time to observe him in his native clime, so to speak. And maybe he'll talk enough to give something away.'

'If indeed he knows anything, Jo,' responded Miss Lucinda. 'But I think you have an excellent idea. Shall we, Beatrice?' She turned to her new best friend (I still couldn't get used to that) for confirmation.

'By all means,' said Miss Bea. 'I'm in the mood for a steak, and I know that the boys would probably appreciate a little cold refreshment with their food.'

The 'boys' nodded in eager agreement, and I sighed. I could handle Derek, I thought, if he got a bit frisky, but I was doubtful that anyone other than Leslie could contain the giant that was LJ. Well, I'd make sure that they had a limit and stuck to it.

With Derek at the wheel – which would certainly not be the case on the way back, I decided firmly – we managed to find our way from the Manchester Police Department to Skinny Joe's Steakhouse and Brewery, only making two wrong turns in the process. Unfortunately, my penchant for carsickness decided to rear its ugly head, and I wasn't too sure about eating anything.

We finally arrived at our destination, Derek pulling the station wagon into a parking space marked 'Take Outs Only'. When I pointed this out to him, still unhappy at his driving, he only shrugged.

'I can't see what the problem is, Jo. It's not like anyone else is going to park there.'

'That's because it's a spot marked for those who are coming to pick up their order,' I said patiently. I swear – men are such boys at times, you know what I mean?

The cool mountain air revived my poor stomach, and I discovered that, yes indeed, I was hungry. *And* I was primed for eavesdropping as well.

Chapter Seventeen

It's amazing how food and drink combine to create an atmosphere of trust, even among those whose trustworthiness is questionable. Skinny Joe's restaurant, and Skinny Joe himself, had perfected the ambience of relaxation, which was welcome after the morning's escapade. Needless to say, I unbent enough to gossip happily alongside my fellow actors, and we found ourselves laughing at nonsense. Of course, a round of beer might have been a factor in our merriment, but who cared? We were having a good time.

I'm not sure when I noticed the occupants of the table nearest the kitchen, but suddenly they stood out in sharp relief against the swinging door. Andy and Bert were hunkered over large plates of food and even larger glasses of beer, and I could feel the heated glares from across the room. Apparently they'd seen us before I'd seen them, giving them more time to work up a bad attitude. When Skinny Joe made an appearance at their table, stained apron and all, he too craned his head around to glower in our direction.

You know how they say you should always be pleasant to the cook and wait staff at an eatery to protect your food order from being, shall we say, tampered with? That went double for Skinny Joe's place, he being both cook and waiter. Of course, the young gal that had seated us, taken our orders, and served us was not to be suspected of sabotage, but I didn't feel too trustful of Joe. I mentally vowed to not ask for anything else, not even water. You never knew.

I nudged Miss Lucinda's arm as inconspicuously as I could, but no such luck. The woman, bless her awkward heart, turned to me and said loudly enough for the occupants of the back table to hear, 'What're you poking my arm for, Jo?'

I was caught in the act and only managed to extract myself by asking for the basket of bread to be passed my way, even though I was full by that time. Leslie, though, gave me a calculating stare, which I returned with one of my own. As if by telepathy, she caught my telegraphed message with her mind and slowly, casually, turned her head to glance over her shoulder. Just as carefully, she turned back toward me and with a slight lifting of her eyebrows let me know that she had spotted Andy and Bert.

After a minute or two had passed, she said, 'I need to run to the ladies' room. You want to go, too, Jo?' Of course I did.

The boys hooted, teasing us about having to travel in packs to use the bathroom.

'What is it with you girls?' asked Derek. 'You never see me asking LJ or anyone else to go to the facilities with me!'

'That's because no one could survive a trip to the bathroom with you, Derek,' I suggested sweetly, causing the rest of the group to burst out laughing. He wrinkled his nose and stuck out his tongue at me, no pretty sight with the bits of food stuck there. Such a boy, I thought, sticking out my tongue right back at him.

I didn't have seven older brothers without learning the fine art of communicating with that particular species.

Leslie and I snaked our way among the tables and

customers, heading for the restrooms which thankfully were located at the opposite side of the restaurant from the kitchen. I don't think I could have casually walked past Andy, Joe, and Bert without being scorched by their eyes.

I waited until Leslie had bent down and checked underneath all three of the enclosed stalls for feet. One could never be too careful, especially when dining in enemy territory.

'I thought,' I began, 'that we had eliminated those three clowns from the suspect list.'

Leslie nodded.

'I did too, but you know what? With the way they're acting, I think we should put them right back on it.'

I agreed with her. Those three, especially Andy, were acting a bit too odd not to be reconsidered. Of course, if being odd was a criterion for identifying a murder suspect, LJ and Miss Lucinda should both be on our list. But that was another matter altogether.

'So what should we do?' whispered Leslie. 'Should we contact Officer Kingsley and tell her?'

'Tell her what? That they're a pack of weirdoes and need to be watched?' I turned to face the mirror, pushing a strand of recalcitrant hair back behind my ear.

'Maybe, if that's what it takes to get the MPD to pay attention to them, sure, why not?' Leslie shrugged her shoulders. 'I think we should also see what else Andy and Bert are doing today. Keep tabs on them.'

'OK. So when they leave, we do too?' I probably looked as skeptical as I felt.

'Yeah. I'm sure we can get the rest of the group to finish up and 'just happen' to leave at the same time.' Leslie's fingers made air quotes, and I nodded. We could do it.

If only Miss Bea's station wagon didn't stick out like

an automotive sore thumb.

With that settled, we strolled back to the table – and gasped *à deux*. Andy and Bert were not there any longer, and from the collective look on the faces of my friends, their departure had not been a friendly one.

'What's going on?' I asked of no one in particular, looking from face to face. 'What did we miss?'

'Oh, not much,' replied Derek in his typical dry manner. 'Just two knuckleheads walking past, giving us the finger and a piece of their minds.'

'Well, they'd best be careful,' I said bitingly. 'They didn't have much mind to begin with.'

I didn't get the usual chuckles, which confirmed to me that this was, indeed, serious business. I turned to Leslie.

'Should we reconsider the spying angle and maybe take this straight back to Officer Kingsley?'

'That's a strong possibility,' she admitted. 'I don't like how this whole thing is going. It feels downright bad, if you get my drift.'

Oh, I got her drift, all right. And I completely agreed. Things were rapidly reversing in a downhill direction, and I didn't want to be the one at the bottom of the heap.

Miss Bea spoke up softly, causing us to strain our ears to hear her. Of course, Skinny Joe was wiping down the table just across from ours, so she was right to be hushed.

'If you all don't mind, I need to go back to the trailer and rest. But if you'd like, you can keep the wagon and sleuth to your hearts' content, provided you make it back by dinner time. Lucy?' She looked enquiringly at Miss Lucinda, who hadn't objected to the use of her nickname.

'I'd probably better join you, Beatrice,' she remarked. 'A rest wouldn't go amiss. And I agree – you kids need to be home by dinner.'

Her tone and words were so parental that I had to grin.

Actually, it felt kind of good, nostalgic even, to be given a curfew. I nodded in agreement, and the others did as well. LJ looked a bit puzzled at Miss Lucinda's words, but I saw Leslie tuck her small arm through his massive one and he settled down. Derek met my eyes and smiled, so I knew he had gotten the same 'mama' vibe as I had felt.

We paid our bill and left the restaurant, eyes squinting a bit in the bright Colorado sunshine. Miss Bea started to hand the keys off to Derek, but a warning grunt from Miss Lucinda made her keep them and climb into the driver's seat. I was relieved, not wanting a showdown with Derek, although he didn't seem too intoxicated. And at least Miss Bea didn't get as lost as Derek did. She drove with her eyes on the road; he fiddled with the radio and his hair.

The drive back to the KOA was silent, but it was a good kind of quiet. We four younger folks were going over the lists of suspects in our heads, adding and subtracting facts. The two elders, the Becklaw gals, were already heading toward that nap. Ah, I thought: the joys of growing older.

With the sisters-in-law safely tucked in for a nap, we left for town again, this time with Leslie at the wheel. She and I'd had about half a beer each, while the boys had consumed a few. I have to admit that she was a competent driver, and we arrived in Manchester safe and sound.

Leslie pulled into the parking lot behind the town's library and cut the engine.

She turned in the seat and smiled at the three of us, reaching across to pat LJ's huge knee.

'Here we are, folks. Now what?'

'Urn, how about comparing what we know, first? That way, we can either break up into pairs or go as a group to wherever it is we're heading,' Derek offered.

That sounded reasonable to me, so I nodded my assent. Leslie did the same, and LJ, after looking at Leslie, nodded as well.

'OK, let's talk about what we know concerning Skinny Joe, Andy's uncle,' Leslie said. 'I'll go first. I know he was in the dressing room with Andy and Bert when Jo and I went to tell them to come out and talk to the police. Right, Jo?' She looked at me for affirmation.

'Yep, that's right,' I replied. 'And I remember someone saying that they saw him out in the parking lot, looking for something near where Josie's – where Josie was.'

Leslie and Derek both gave me a strange look.

'What?' I asked. 'Didn't someone say that?'

'Er, Jo, that was you. You told us that *you* saw Skinny Joe in the parking lot,' Leslie replied, her eyes looking at me with concern. 'Are you OK? I mean, did you need a rest, too?'

I groaned inwardly while trying to maintain a neutral expression. It would not do for them to think that craziness was a constant issue with me, barring occasional incidents with furry creatures.

'Oops, my bad,' I said with what I hoped was a 'silly me' smile. I did everything but slap myself on the forehead.

'Yeah, OK,' said Derek. 'Let's focus, shall we?'

I reverted to childhood, sticking my tongue out at Derek. He was a fine one to talk, I thought. Like he was Mr Perfect or something.

'Now, now,' said Leslie, stepping into Miss Bea's role as the peacemaker. 'Let's work together, OK, folks?'

Her perky smile was too much for me. Well, what can I say? I'm an equal opportunity kind of gal, so I stuck my tongue out at her as well.

Chapter Eighteen

I'm not sure how we finally got it all together, but we managed. By the time we finished comparing lists and ideas, it had boiled down to two possible suspects: Julian and Lily. We decided to concentrate on Julian Sweet.

Julian I could almost understand. He had done a complete disappearing act from the fairgrounds that night, even though Andy and Bert swore he had pulled in right after them. We'd worked out the timing, realizing that, yes indeed, Julian might have been in the same place as Josie at the same time. What their connection was, though, I still didn't get. Why he'd want to kill her was a huge part of the mystery.

That was going to be Derek's job to figure out. He was going to start in the library, of all places, saying that these were hotbeds of gossip in small towns like Manchester. Now that I could readily accept, coming from the Grand Central Station for Gossip myself. You could never keep a secret for long in Piney Woods, and by the time it got back to you, it was almost unrecognizable with all the embellishments.

The rest of us – LJ, Leslie, and I – were going to find out where Julian had been since the murder. I don't know if anyone had thought to find this out, so step one was to get his home address. We were going to the library as well, for the local phone directory.

Making sure the station wagon was locked and keys safely deposited in her jeans pocket, Leslie led the way into the little library. It, of course, was built in the log cabin style that I was beginning to associate with Colorado. It had a large portico with a jutting roof over the double front doors that provided its patrons with some means of shelter from the snow or rain, depending on the season. I mentally compared this building to our own Piney Woods version, surprised to find they were similar, faux log walls excepted. Since the climate could be rather damp in Louisiana, especially during the spring and summer months, covered parking and doorways were coveted.

It was brightly lit inside, and I found myself looking around at the stacks of books with longing. If only I had time to browse, I thought. Reading for pleasure was one of my favorite pastimes, and this was a treasure trove. Alas, I was only here to track a potential killer's movements. I followed Leslie and LJ to the information desk, giving the books one more glance over my shoulder.

A pleasant-looking woman sat on the other side of the desk, tortoiseshell readers perched on the end of a rather pert little nose. She fit the image of the typical librarian, I thought idly, noticing the tailored blouse and skirt, and the sensible flats, when she emerged from behind the desk to lead us over to the section that housed the telephone directories of Silverton County.

'Now you just let me know if there is anything I can do to help you folks, OK? We're down a librarian today, but I'm sure someone will be available if you need us.' She smiled as she said this, then began to turn back to her desk.

'Excuse me?' I began, and she stopped in her tracks. the pleasant smile back on her face. 'You said that you are missing one librarian. Would that be Lily, by any chance?'

She looked a bit startled, then said, 'Why, yes. Yes, it

is. Are you a friend of hers?'

I thought quickly. Maybe, if I said I knew her, we could get the scoop on Lily as well as Julian, killing the proverbial two birds with one library visit.

'Yes. I'm in town for just a few more days and I had wanted to say hello to her. Is she out for the day? I could come back tomorrow.' I smiled my most brilliant 'you can trust me' smile at her, hoping to cover my lies in friendliness.

It worked. She hesitated but an instant, then crooked her finger at me. 'Follow me and I'll check her schedule. It'll take just a second.'

We paraded behind her, back to the information desk where she reached into a drawer and pulled out a book marked 'Schedules'. She flipped over a few pages then ran her forefinger down until she found the name she was looking for. A frown appeared on her face, the tiny wrinkles pushing the readers even further down her nose.

'Hmm. I see that Lily has not been here since,' – she ran her finger across the page – 'since last Friday. Very unusual for her. Let me check something first.'

She turned her back to us and picked up the receiver of a standard-issue office phone. Pressing buttons rapidly, she listened briefly then replaced the receiver.

'I just called her extension just in case she was on vacation or something and had left a notification.' The librarian looked troubled. 'It says that she is out of the office indefinitely on personal leave. I'm sorry, folks. I didn't know anything about that.'

I thought for minute, then took a risk. 'Is there a chance that you can give me her address? Or her cellphone number? I realize it's probably against your policy, but Lily is one of my closest friends and I told her that I'd be in town this week.' The moment the words left my mouth I could have kicked myself. If she was that good a friend, shouldn't I already have this information?

Thankfully, the librarian was upset enough not to notice my verbal gaff. She hesitated only a fraction then reached inside her desk for a small book. She laid it on the desk, then said,

'I can't give you any personal information, I'm afraid. Even if Lily is a friend. I'm sorry.'

With that she walked from behind the desk.

We three stared at each other, but only for a second. I reached down and grabbed up the book, flipping rapidly through the pages. I found Lily under the 'T's. Lily Thompson, I read. Well, if nothing else, we at least now had a last name. Quickly, I copied down the information, laying the book back on the desk. I smiled to myself. If this was detecting, it was a piece of cake.

Oh, how wrong I was. At that moment, though, I was confident. I could find Lily, figure out the reasons behind her odd behavior (and yes, breaking and entering definitely fell under 'odd behavior'), and nail her if she was Josie's killer.

Derek joined us near the front door. I could tell by the look of frustration on his face that he had not been as successful as we had. I was loath to brag, though, so I let Leslie do it. I had no interest in another verbal entanglement with anyone, and I was still flying high from my discovery.

'Good for you,' was Derek's terse reply to Leslie's cheery commentary on Lily and her possible whereabouts. Talk about your sour grapes! Derek's face was going to atrophy into a pucker if he kept this up. I couldn't help myself. I leaned over and gave his arm a little saccharine pat that said, 'It's OK, buddy.'

His scowl could have scared Frankenstein's monster. Score!

We trooped back to the station wagon, Leslie and I chatting, and LJ following behind Leslie like an overgrown pet. Derek walked at the rear, scuffing the ground with the toe of his tennis shoes. Well, I'd have to find out just what had made Mr Sunshine such a gloomy little rain cloud. I fell into step beside him.

'So what's up, Derek?' I asked as we walked back to the car. I aimed for a light tone with an underpinning of 'innocent'.

He sent me a sideways glare but I'd already thrown up the laser shields. I beamed back at him. I maintained my silence, counting on the adage that a vacuum must be filled by necessity. He filled it, all right.

I will not write the exact wording he used, this being a family-friendly tale. However, I will paraphrase:

Derek had approached a young library worker who was returning books to the shelves. She was cute and blonde, and apparently well aware of her attributes. Derek's attempts at suave conversation had toppled right over, landing in a heap of mangled words and embarrassment. He hadn't stayed around for her response. But he had heard her giggling as he stomped out of the stacks. He hadn't even gotten to first base with his information-gathering expedition.

In spite of the ridiculousness of it all, I actually felt sorry for the guy. Having as many brothers as I do, I know what injured masculine pride does to the fragile male ego.

'Never mind,' I said briskly. 'We've got something to follow up on Lily, so that should keep us busy today. By the way, her last name is Thompson.'

Derek stopped walking and looked at me with an odd expression in his eyes. 'Thompson? Are you sure?'

I stared back at him. 'Of course I'm sure! I got her name from the librarian's address book. Why?'

'Because that's what I heard someone calling Skinny Joe. Thompson, I mean. As in "Skinny Joe Thompson".'

My mouth made an 'O' of surprise.

'Are you sure? Then that would make Lily Andy's cousin or something, since Skinny Joe's his uncle.'

This was becoming a hodgepodge of confusion. Were these people all related or something? And how come we hadn't known that to begin with? It wasn't like it was a state secret.

We caught up to Leslie and LJ, who had been standing next to Miss Bea's pride and joy, watching us with curiosity.

Derek spoke first, filling them in on the possible relationship between Lily, Andy, and Skinny Joe. Leslie looked interested, and LJ looked puzzled. I could almost hear his brain whirring as it struggled to make the connections.

'So it's a possibility that Lily had something to do with this mess, especially since she's done a runner,' Derek concluded.

I had to concur. Nothing else made sense.

'So what's our next move?' Leslie asked, one arm tucked through LJ's.

'Well, I think we need to find her house – we've got the address now – and see if she's there. If she's not, then I think that we'll have to talk to Andy. Or Skinny Joe,' replied Derek.

I made a face. Neither aspect thrilled me, especially since I clearly recalled the looks on their faces at the restaurant. They didn't look too happy, to say the least. Needs must when the Devil drives, as my mother would say, whatever *that* little gem meant. But I remembered she would say it whenever she had anything that she didn't want to do, so it must be apropos for this occasion.

'All righty then,' I said. 'Let's hit the road. It can't be that hard to find.'

Actually, that was a true statement, not a pipe dream. Manchester was the most simply laid out town I had ever seen. Apparently the employee with the dullest imagination had been called upon to design the naming system, and it was most likely a man who had better things to do with his time, like skip out early for bowling. All streets running north to south were numbers, and all streets running east to west were letters.

The main street of the town which ran east to west was called Main. This was crossed by Center, running north to south, forming the exact middle of the town. All roads in the upper right quadrant of the plan were 'Avenues', as in 1st Avenue and C Avenue. The streets in the lower right quadrant were 'Streets'. The lower left quadrant roads were 'Places' and the remaining quadrant had 'Roads'. So it stood to reason that if the address listed for Lily Thompson was 255 East 'A' Place, she must live south-west of Main and Center.

With me giving directions and Leslie doing a fine job behind the wheel, we found Lily's tiny bungalow without a hitch.

The driveway was gravel-filled and rough, looking as though it had not been tended to for a while. A few scruffy-looking forsythia bushes clung to the sides of a tiny railed-in front porch, and the ash tree in the middle of the front lawn looked dehydrated. Not the sort of place I'd have pictured someone like Lily living in, especially since she came across as neat and organized. Maybe she just didn't have a green thumb, I reasoned. Lord knows I don't. Give me a potted plant and I can kill it in four days flat – sooner, if it has flowers.

Leslie had pulled into the driveway; bumping across

ruts in the dirt. We sat in the car, waiting for one of us to volunteer to get out and knock on the door. Actually, the three of them looked at me, waiting for me to offer to do it, so with a deep sigh of martyrdom, I did so, slamming the car door for emphasis. The things I do to keep folks happy!

I marched myself straight to the front door, knocking on it and simultaneously ringing the bell. Between each round I listened closely for any sound from inside. After three attempts, I looked back toward the car filled with expectant faces and shrugged exaggeratedly. Derek stuck his head out of the passenger window and suggested I peek through a window or two.

In turn, I suggested that he – well, it doesn't really matter what I suggested, dear reader. Believe me when I say that it was enough to get him out of the car, bad attitude firmly back in place.

Together we walked around the house's perimeter, alternately peering through dust-coated windows and making snippy comments to one another. It was enough to stay my homesickness, if I had any; I felt like I was fighting with one of my brothers.

It must have been the next-to-last window when I began to feel a familiar flutter of anxiety in my gut. Something did not feel right. I motioned Derek to go ahead of me, and I hung back, waiting to see what he found, if anything. I crossed my fingers for the latter.

I really must learn the art of crossing fingers. It didn't work, in the biggest way.

Chapter Nineteen

The look on Derek's face was eloquent, no need for words. Which was a good thing, since he wasn't up to much speaking right now.

He had peeked through that last window, cupping his hands around his eyes in an effort to combat glare and dust. He must have been able to see just fine, because he seemed to spring back from the window as if on an invisible pulley. I reached out a hand to steady him, and I could tell that this was not going to be good. At all.

Together we retraced our path back to the station wagon where Leslie and LJ sat cuddled together like a mama bear and her rather overgrown, overstuffed cub. The silence in our approach was more an alert than if we had been screeching, because Leslie sat straight up and stepped out of the car door.

'What?' Her eyes swept back and forth from me to Derek, trying to read our faces. 'What did you see?'

Derek swallowed hard. I'll give him this: he can be as vulnerable as the next person. A feeling of protection fluttered around in my chest; he reminded me so much of a little boy who had just seen something that would scar him for life.

I slipped an arm though his, then spoke up. 'I'm not too sure what Derek saw, but let's give him a minute to get his thoughts together. Do we still have those water bottles in the back of the wagon?' In times of dire emergency, my mother had always plied us with food or drink and I had learned from her. A water bottle was better than nothing at this point.

Leslie walked around to the back of the car, pulling up on the handle that opened the hatchback. She leaned in and rummaged about, returning to us in triumph: she had found two water bottles, a carton of juice, and a small bag of chocolate-covered raisins. I gave Derek the juice and the raisins. Sugar was a sure-fire cure for whatever ailed you.

I twisted open the cap of one of the water bottles, taking a long draw on the tepid water. Derek had tossed a handful of the raisins into his mouth and was in the process of washing them down with the juice. I judged that he was fit to speak, going by his returning color.

'OK, Derek. Nice and slow – what did you see back there?' I spoke in as kindly a tone as I could, the little boy image still clear in my mind.

He swallowed the juice and raisin combo, sputtering a bit, but he didn't seem as upset as before. 'I'm pretty sure it's Lily,' he said simply.

I groaned. This was exactly what I had been feeling, had been dreading. Not only did this cut the suspect list down even further, it also turned our killer into more of a menace.

Leslie took over, saying briskly, 'OK. First things first. I'll call the Manchester Police Department. Derek, you have a seat in the car with LJ, keep each other company. Jo, you come with me to the backyard. We need to see this for ourselves.' She turned and began walking determinedly toward the back of the tiny house, me on her heels and protesting.

'Look here, Leslie. I've seen one dead body. I really don't need to see another.'

'We don't even know if she's dead,' Leslie replied in a tone that one might employ with a person whose marbles might not be all there. 'Let's take a look. She might just be ill, or hurt. That way we'll have good info for the PD, OK?'

That did make sense, I had to admit. Still, I silently volunteered her to be the one to determine Lily's current state.

We approached that last window, and I hung back just enough to let Leslie step ahead of me. She did much as Derek had, cupping her hands against the dirty pane in order to shield her eyes from the morning glare. There the similarities stopped, though. Leslie continued to stare inside, her mouth open in a parody of surprise. Stepping back from the window as carefully as if walking on glass, Leslie looked at me.

'She's in there, all right. And I think it's safe to report that Lily Thompson is deceased.'

From her tone, I thought it better not to ask for details. Those could wait for the police report.

Leslie made the requisite call to the Manchester Police Department, and they arrived in due course. I was glad to see our Officer Kingsley among those milling around the tiny yard, stringing up the yellow crime tape and taking pictures. I guess it always amazes me just how many folks it takes to investigate a crime. I'd always thought it was just like you saw in the movies, all the bit-parters; the kind that Miss Bea loved to hire.

Anyhow, I debated whether or not to hang about to see Lily's body being carried out and hauled off. I wanted to see her for myself. I'm not even sure why, but I did. Leslie and Derek had already given their statements to the officer and I had been told to wait for someone to talk to me.

Being the enterprising young woman that I am, I decided to speed things up a bit; to find an investigator to talk to and discover the particulars of the murder. I strolled around the back of the house, ducking under the yellow barrier, and caught a glimpse of Officer Kingsley standing just outside the back door. I raised my hand in a slight wave, hoping to catch her eye without making a big fuss.

I was in luck. Officer Kingsley saw me and snapped closed the cellphone she had been talking on, waving at me to join her. I did, walking across the backyard with its worn-out grass and empty flowerpots. The back door stood ajar, the room bustling with activity. I craned my neck to see around Officer K, but she quickly put an arm across the doorway.

'You don't need to see, Jo,' she admonished me. 'It's not a pretty sight.'

I looked up at her, eyebrows raised in question. 'Is it really that bad?'

Officer Kingsley nodded her head somberly. 'It is. Take my word for it, OK?'

I said that I would, but I made a note to talk to Leslie and Derek. It was share and share alike, as far as I was concerned.

Officer K took down a few statements from me. I told her how we got the address, told her that we decided to check it out ourselves, and that Leslie had driven us over.

'That's about it,' I added. 'I got out and pounded on the door a couple of times, then Derek and I started looking through windows. When he came to the last one, Derek spotted Lily. Then Leslie peeped in after and confirmed it. We called you. That's it.'

Officer Kingsley closed her notebook, reminding me not to talk about anything to do with the crime, and to give her a call if anything else came to mind. I agreed then walked back to the station wagon.

Leslie and LJ were in the back seat, his massive arm

curled around her shoulders. She did not look good, I thought worriedly, wondering just how bad Lily had looked. Derek, seeming somewhat on his way to recovery, had slipped in to the front passenger seat. I rolled my eyes. That meant only one thing; *I* had to drive.

Well, I've never been one to shirk my duty, even if it included piloting a yacht-sized station wagon, replete with faux wood paneling and three passengers in various stages of quiet. I took the keys from Leslie, inserted them into the ignition, and turned. The engine roared into life and we were off, the ancient steering wheel held tightly in my grasp.

I debated starting a conversation with Derek, but a sideways glance told me he was still in no frame of mind for talk of any sort, so I refrained. I reached for the radio's controls, and Miss Bea's choice in music came blasting through the speakers. It had amused me when I found out her penchant for classic rock, but I figured that now was not the time to be critical. Any noise was better than no noise.

Unless it was Queen's "Death on Two Legs". We did *not* need any reminder of death and mayhem, so I quickly clicked the radio off.

OK, I thought grimly. This was too much. Sure, Derek and Leslie might have seen something terrible through that window, but didn't they have the responsibility to share? I decided to take the bull by the horns and cleared my throat.

'Derek. Leslie. I don't want to upset you, but I really, truly want to know what you saw in that house.' I caught Leslie's eye in the rearview mirror, and almost took my words back.

Almost. I develop an insatiable curiosity when anyone doesn't want to share with me. I soldiered on.

'Derek. You first. Where was Lily at when you saw

her?' I figured a direct question would prod him into speech.

He cut his eyes at me, then turned back to look out of the window. 'Why do you want to know so badly?' He turned back to look at me. My eyes were fixed on the curving road ahead of us, but I could feel his stare.

'I just do, that's why,' I retorted. 'Besides, aren't we part of a team here? You know what they say: "There's no 'I' in team".' That should get the point across, I thought smugly, as I navigated the road.

'Maybe not, but there *is* a "me" and this "me" doesn't feel much like talking, OK?'

Humph, I thought. Well, I'd worm it out of him one way or another. Tucking that into the back of my mind, I guided the lumbering station wagon through the opened gates of the KOA.

I dropped the boys off at their trailer then drove to ours. A glance in the rearview mirror showed LJ leading Derek up to the door with one beefy hand on Derek's slight shoulder. That made me feel a bit better. LJ and I would probably be playing nursemaid this evening, but that was OK. Leslie and Derek would do as much for us.

Miss Bea and Miss Lucinda should be awake by now, I thought. I wanted to get some food into Leslie, maybe get her to cough it up – what she had seen, I mean, not the food. The front door was locked but I had a key. Opening the door, I let us in, calling out, 'Miss Lucinda? Miss Bea? We're back!'

A faint snoring came down the hallway, and I grinned. The old dears were sawing logs. Well, a few more minutes in bed probably wouldn't hurt. I'd take care of Leslie then wake them up. I led her into the kitchen, not even thinking about Lily at the moment.

Leslie was, though. She stopped cold in the doorway, not wanting to walk in. I had already opened the refrigerator and taken out the carton of milk and a piece of leftover cheesecake, intending to feed her.

She didn't answer. Her eyes, fixed on the small kitchen table, were filled with tears.

'Leslie? What's wrong?' I hurriedly set the milk and dessert down on the counter, putting an arm around her shoulders.

'It was so awful,' she sobbed. 'You can't even begin to imagine.' I let her cry for a few minutes.

'Do you want to talk about it?' I asked gently. Yes, you do, I silently encouraged her. This was my chance to find out just what had shaken Derek and her so much.

She stayed silent, focused on some point in time that only she could see. I was beginning to think she had gone catatonic on me, then she spoke.

'She must have made someone really, really angry,' Leslie said softly, still fixed on some distant point.

I waited for more, but that was it. Sometimes you just have to use a cattle prod, I thought, and this was one of those times.

'Leslie? Did they do something else to her, besides kill her?' Oh, boy. What could be worse than being killed? Jo, you are a brilliant conversationalist at times, I scolded myself.

'Yes.' Her answer surprised me. I suppose I expected her to give me a dirty look, not a response.

'What do you mean? Exactly?' I prompted her.

She looked me full in the face then, her eyes widening at the horror of what she had seen. *What* Leslie had seen?

'Jo, they – they cut out her tongue!' With that, she slumped back, tears filling her eyes.

I stared at her, not sure if what I thought I'd heard and what she had said where a match. 'Her tongue, as in what's in your mouth? *That* tongue?'

In spite of the idiocy of the question, Leslie nodded. Her face and neck were wet with crying, and I reached out to hug her close. No wonder the poor girl had gone semi-comatose.

'That wasn't all, either,' she continued, her voice muffled against my shoulder. I stiffened. What else had they done to that poor girl?

'She was sitting at her table just like she was eating dinner, only ...' Leslie got quieter. 'It wasn't food that was on her plate.'

I closed my eyes, trying not to picture what she had told me. Too late; the image was firmly fixed in my mind. I could see Lily, her pretty face demoralized with the damage to her mouth, the plate of – well, I wasn't going there. Not now.

Not sure of what to say next, I gave her a final squeeze and backed away from her. 'Look, Leslie. I want you to sit down. I'll make you some hot tea and then I'm going to wake Miss Bea and Miss Lucinda. I think they should be in on this as well.'

Chapter Twenty

I've been trying to place the look on the Becklaw women's faces when they got the full gist of Leslie's story. Looking back, I can recall a mixture of repugnance and fear, but something else was there as well. The closest I can get to it is the way people act when they see a bad car accident: they don't want to look, but they can't help it. The Becklaw gals were certainly in that category.

Once I had assured them that yes, Derek was being cared for by LJ, and that no, I hadn't seen it, only Leslie, Miss Bea went into mother mode, murmuring over Leslie as if she had been the victim and not Lily. Miss Lucinda, the more pragmatic of the two, stomped into the kitchen and began banging pots and pans around, or at least that's what it sounded like. Her mantra said that food was the best cure for shock, and with a shock as great as Leslie's, we were going to be feasting tonight.

The thought of sitting down at the table, however, turned my stomach. It would probably be better if we ate in the tiny living room on trays, especially since the only table we had to use was a kitchen table. I shuddered. There was no telling how long I would have to avoid eating in a kitchen.

I ventured in, ready to duck a flying pan or two. Leslie was being cared for, Miss Bea was occupied, and that left me to my own devices. I figured that playing *sous-chef* to

Miss Lucinda was much better than reliving the day over and over in the solitude of my room.

Miss Lucinda was bent over the cutting board, wielding a paring knife and slicing a yellow onion as if she had the killer in her sights.

Without looking up at me, she said 'Get me the chicken from the refrigerator. I thawed it out last night, and it's a good thing I did. We need some comfort food around here and I'm going to make Bolstering Chicken Stew.' She continued to chop and dice the heck out of that onion.

'Oh, and grab the carrots from the veggie rack. You'll need to slice those up fairly thin, along with a couple celery stalks.'

Those tasks kept us busy, working in silence, a heady *mélange* of aromas filling the air. The chicken was set to boil in a pot of water and broth mixture, and the chopped veggies followed. Miss Lucinda then added several cans of drained white beans and a can of diced tomatoes, judicious amounts of pepper and garlic salt, covering the whole thing with a tight lid. She nodded in satisfaction.

'We'll let that come to a boil, then cut the fire down just a hair to let it simmer for about half an hour. In the meantime, see if you can rustle up some bread or rolls.'

I do enjoy baking and cooking, and I just happened to have memorized my favorite recipe for home-made bread called Easy-Peasy Bread. By the time the stew had simmered and the bread had baked, the entire trailer smelled heavenly. I completely understood why food could be so comforting.

Carrying filled bowls and slices of bread out to the living room, the four of us concentrated on eating and relaxing. I noticed that Leslie looked much calmer than she had an hour before; Miss Bea's motherly ministrations had obviously done the trick. I idly wondered how Derek and LJ were getting along, and it was as if my thoughts had pulled them down our way. Within a minute or two, they stood on the trailer's small porch, knocking on the door.

Installed in the living room with stew and bread, the two boys ate rapidly and silently. It has always seemed to me that boys of any age can become hungry on demand, and these two were certainly proving my theory. Between the six of us, we decimated the Bolstering Chicken Stew and the Easy-Peasy Bread, empty bowls set aside on the floor near our respective feet. It was time to talk.

LJ had managed to insinuate his bulk onto the couch between Miss Bea and Leslie, and the three of them looked as tightly fitted together as a dovetailed drawer. Derek sat on the floor, leaning back against the wall, Miss Lucinda was in the chair nearest the kitchen, and I sat in the matching one placed by the door. Anyone who walked by and casually peeked inside would have thought that we were a family relaxing together after dinner, nothing more on our minds than what to do the next day.

How wrong they would have been.

Somehow – probably due to the calming influence of the chicken stew – we managed to talk it out, creating a probable timeline for Lily's movements between the aborted performance and the finding of her body. As far as we knew, Andy and Skinny Joe were now both bereaved family members as well as suspects, and Julian had fallen off the cops' collective radar. That seemed to make the most sense, at least to me. By putting together earlier statements of Joe's odd behavior at the first crime scene, and the fact that Lily's relationship to him had not been divulged (although Andy's had), I was beginning to think that something along the lines of a family feud was at the bottom of this. Family issues were notorious for wreaking havoc and even murder.

That didn't explain Josie, though, I had to admit. It

could be that the two murders were not related at all, and that it had been a random crime. But then I would go back to Skinny Joe's behavior, and the entire thing would look connected again. What a mess! I had no idea how detectives were able to make sense of anything as crazy as these two crimes. My hope was that someone would be able to unravel this entire fiasco, and soon.

Our reservations ran out the day after tomorrow.

Over dishes of coffee ice cream, we hashed out a plan. I voted for staying on a few more days – just to see the thing through, I explained. I was also hoping to do a bit more detecting, although without today's grim result. Leslie and Derek seconded the motion, and Miss Bea, looking doubtful, listened to our reasoning.

To my complete surprise, Miss Lucinda offered to foot the bill for another week's lodging at the KOA. Miss Bea promptly snapped up the offer, and a re-energized Leslie and LJ were sent to see the McLaughlins about extending our stay. The worst case scenario, I thought, was a transfer back to the YMCA, which wouldn't be so bad either. And much, much closer to that yummy restaurant.

While the twosome went about their errand, I suggested to Miss Bea that we make a call to Officer Kingsley sometime that evening. I wanted to know if there was anything else on Julian, even though he was more than likely off the suspect list. There was still a niggling in the back of my mind that I couldn't shake, and it was somehow connected with him.

Derek protested, saying that more than likely the officer would be working on the two murders, looking for linkage there. I agreed, but still pushed the idea of making that call. Miss Bea's firm voice, though, made the decision for me.

'We need to let today's incident find a place in our minds first, dear Jo, before we add to the burden, don't you think? And besides, if we sleep on what we already know, something may come to us in the morning.' She smiled kindly at me, much as a teacher would at an eager student forging ahead without a logical plan.

So, once the reservations had been renewed – the McLaughlins were delighted to keep us, as most of this week's visitors would be leaving next day – we settled in for the evening, each one in his or her own room, or, in the case of the Becklaw women, to their shared abode.

I had packed a book, thinking that I would have some time to read on the road. It is the best way, I have found, to get relaxed and drowsy, especially when sleeping in a strange bed. Unfortunately, my choice may not have been the most logical in this situation; it was thrilling, suspenseful, and laced with a murder or two. I tried to read, I really did. Finally, though, I had to give up. My mind was playing tricks on me, substituting names and descriptions until I couldn't tell if I was reading about a fictitious crime or the ones in which I had become involved.

I had taken my cellphone out in case my mother tried to ring. She seemed to have a sixth sense when it came to calling me; it was generally at the most inopportune moments when I couldn't talk, and she would accuse me of not having time for her. Setting my book aside, I picked up the phone, toying with the idea of calling Officer Kingsley. I know that I had agreed to leave it until the morning, but …

I'm not known for my impulse-control abilities. I got up and re-dressed in the clothes I had taken off and tossed on the chair near my bed, reaching for the shoes I had kicked out of the way. I hadn't planned on going out again, but some instinct pushed me to be ready for anything. Digging into my jeans pocket, I found the card that Officer K had given me. It only took a brief second to make up my mind. I dialed.

The recorded music on the other end of the line brought a wry smile to my lips: Officer Kingsley's choice was the bouncy anthem of the 1980s and Bobby McFerrin's cheery voice encouraged me to 'Don't Worry, Be Happy.' I shook my head. Not worrying was the farthest thing from my mind at the moment.

'Kingsley here.' The firm voice of the detective sounded in my ear. I paused, forgetting why I had called. 'Hello? This is Officer Kingsley. Can I help you?' This time my mind kicked into gear.

'This is Jo, Jo Anderson. I'm part of Becklaw's.' I waited to see if she remembered me.

'Yes, of course. Is everything OK?' Her concern sounded genuine, encouraging me to talk.

'Well, yes and no. We were still a little shook up over what we found, er ... over finding Lily today, but I think we'll survive. I was just thinking,' I went on, 'about Julian Sweet. Is he – I mean, do you still consider him to be involved? You know, as a suspect?' I held my breath, waiting for the officer to tell me to take a hike, to mind my own business.

The silence on the other end was palpable. I could feel her hesitation, and I mentally willed her to spill the beans. My telepathy skills must have gotten stronger.

'Well,' Officer Kingsley said, 'Yes. And no. I personally have feeling that he is part of this, but personal feelings aren't court worthy, you know? I still need proof of involvement before making an arrest of any kind, and so far, nothing doing.'

I let out my breath. 'I see.' I replied. 'Of course. That makes perfect sense. It's just that ...' I broke off, not finishing my sentence.

'So, if you know something that would be helpful, tell

me.' Her voice was now authoritative, in investigator mode.

'Well, that's just it. I have some feelings of my own that I can't explain. I keep thinking back to the day we found Josie, the way that Julian was there and then he wasn't. It's just, I don't know, *odd*, I guess.' I could hear the uncertainty in my voice.

Officer Kingsley was silent. I could almost hear the wheels turning in her mind. What she said next surprised me into full wakefulness.

'I tell you what, Jo. I'm leaving the station now. How about we meet for coffee and a talk? My treat.'

I hesitated but a second. 'Sure. You name the place, I'll be there.'

I have never actually stolen a car before, nor, to the best of my knowledge, ridden with anyone who has. Technically, I stole Miss Bea's car. Logically, I borrowed it. After all, I was on my way to gather more information for the good of the troupe, wasn't I?

Chapter Twenty-one

I eased the car out of the KOA driveway and onto the main road that led back to Manchester. Officer Kingsley had suggested that we meet at the town's only all-night diner, located just down the block from Skinny Joe's Steakhouse and Brewery. When I arrived, she was already there – no surprise, since the police station was literally just around the corner.

A steaming mug of coffee already sat on my side of the Formica-topped table, badly scarred with years of use. I slid into the booth, giving Officer Kingsley what I hoped was a confident grin. Lord only knew what I'd say if she asked me about the car situation.

'How's it going?' I asked her casually, taking an experimental sip of the coffee. My past experiences with diner coffee have ranged from the sublime to downright sinful. Some of the stuff touted as coffee could have been used to clean car batteries. This was somewhere between 'edge of bitter' and 'paint thinner', but I didn't complain. A coffee mug can be used as a prop for nervous hands, I've found.

On the table, Officer K laid a bulging notebook, ubiquitous pen clipped to its cover. She patted it.

'I brought along every note I've taken on the two murders, including some my other detectives made as well. It's clear to me that Julian Sweet is not a suspect, at least not on paper.'

She paused to sip her own coffee, making a face that expressed her opinion. Apparently Officer Kingsley didn't mind drinking a brew akin to turpentine, though; she took a follow-up drink, setting the mug down hard enough to slop a bit over the edge.

I thought about that for a moment, faking another sip. There was no way in the world I was drinking that mess.

'I know that no one has anything evidence-wise against Julian. I *know* that, Officer Kingsley. It's just that, like I said, something isn't jiving when I think about him.' I shrugged, looking at the tabletop.

'Sometimes feelings are the only thing that a detective has to go on, Jo,' she replied gently. 'Unfortunately, like I said on the phone, feelings don't stand up in court.'

'If you were me,' I asked, looking directly at her, 'where would you start? I mean, if you were going off a feeling?'

Officer Kingsley didn't drop my gaze. In fact, she looked a tad amused at my enthusiasm. Well, as Crazy Great-Aunt Opal would say, "Foolish is as foolish does." And boy, was I ever getting ready to be Grade A Foolish. Crazy Great-Aunt Opal also said, "You gotta clean up your own mess", which actually did make a lot of sense. Jo, I told myself firmly, get on with the foolishness. There was certainly a mess here that needed some cleaning.

'Officer Kingsley,' I began confidently, 'I believe I can help you turn the feeling into fact.'

Her amusement was not veiled at this remark. Actually, she threw her head back and barked out a short laugh, causing the lone waitress to cast worried glances in our direction. I think I must have looked worried as well, because Officer Kingsley stopped laughing and stared at me. She appeared to be sizing me up. Or, at the very least, assessing my comment.

'Look,' I interjected. 'I know I don't know much about detecting. Or much about acting, for that matter. But I'm willing to try, and I really think that someone needs to take Julian seriously. There has to be some reason why he was there and then he wasn't, and then Josie was dead. It just fits, to my mind.'

I know I sounded stubborn. It was one of my finest qualities, I felt, and I could put it to good use when I chose.

Shaking her head, Officer Kingsley lifted the coffee to her lips in an automatic gesture.

'Dang it all to heck!' Coffee dripped off her chin and down the front of her shirt. Not a smart move, I thought, trying to shake your head and drink at the same time. 'This was my last unstained shirt. Great.' She sighed, looking at me as if I had caused it. 'Jo, since you'll probably do some nosing around anyway, regardless of what I say, I'll do this much for you: you try to find out what motive Julian might have had, and I'll keep looking at his movements. Fair enough?'

Absolutely. I could do that. After all, I had five other folks backing me up on this one, and since six heads are much better than one, we'd surely find out something. We said our goodbyes, me promising to keep my head down and she commenting that I d better or she'd lose her job.

The drive back to the KOA seemed shorter; my mind was whirling with the new approach. Finding the motive seemed logical, the first place we should have looked, but I think the shock of seeing two murdered bodies had driven that aspect from our collective minds.

I suppose that I should not have been surprised to see the Becklaw Wall of Censure facing me in the living room. Perched together on the sofa, the sisters-in-law were the perfect exemplar of parental disapproval, mouths set in tight lines and arms folded across well-padded bosoms.

'Er … hi, there,' I began lamely. No answer from The Wall, just twin glares of indignation.

I tried again. 'Miss Bea and Miss Lucinda, I didn't want to wake you …' And that was as far as I got. Hurricane Beatrice made landfall with Category 5 status.

'I have been sitting here worrying myself sick, Josephine.' Uh oh, I thought. I knew from experience that when someone used my entire name, trouble was in the offing. 'And how do you think I felt hearing you sneaking out of the house, with the car keys to boot?' She was almost quivering, she was so angry at me.

'Miss Bea,' I began. She didn't give me a chance.

The Becklaw Tag Team swung into action. For the next few minutes, they took turns berating me, scolding me, and imploring me to tell them what they had done to make me act this way. Good grief! I had an easier time explaining myself to my seven over-protective brothers. When they finally stopped for a breather, I spoke.

'Miss Bea. Miss Lucinda. I didn't "sneak" out, really. I truly thought you were asleep. And I didn't mean to do anything to lose your trust or make you mad.' I walked over to them and squatted in front of them, my hands on their arms. 'I met Officer Kingsley for coffee. She's agreed to let us help. In fact, she's given us a job.'

I let the words sink in for a moment, still looking up into their sleep-lined faces.

In spite of their ire, I could feel their anxiety for me. What remarkable women they were, both strong in their own way. I mentally reclassified them as Amazonians.

Miss Lucinda gave in first. Pushing a strand of lavender hair from her eyes, she reached over and patted my hand.

'Well, that's a horse of a different color altogether,' she declared. 'Isn't it, Beatrice?'

She gave a sharp nudge in the side to the smaller

Becklaw gal, who returned the poke with one of her own.

'Oh, quit, Lucinda. I know when I'm beat.' Miss Bea's words were testy but the smile on her sweet face was like sunshine. Ah. Forgiven.

'Look, it's really late. And I want Leslie and the boys here to listen as well, so maybe we could talk about this in the morning?' I made the request into a question, knowing my limits of grace.

They both nodded graciously at me. Their regal manner could put Queen Elizabeth's to shame. I almost started looking around for the Royal Handbag.

Needless to say, I slept like a log. I was going to say 'like the dead', but I was really starting to have issues with that word. At any rate, my sleep was deep and dreamless, and I awoke feeling more refreshed than I had for a while. My roomies were already breakfasting on toasted English muffins thickly spread with real butter and local honey, and a covered teapot sat in the middle of the table. A quick look at Leslie reassured me that she seemed to be OK with eating in the kitchen. I must admit to being a tad worried over that aspect of the case.

'Good morning,' I said brightly as I slipped into the empty chair between Miss Bea and Leslie. 'Could you pass the butter, please?'

I spent the next few minutes in contented grazing, almost inhaling the first muffin. I had awakened starving, no doubt the result of my late night. At last, sated and happy, I leaned back in my chair and looked around at the three women.

'So, I thought perhaps we could get a quick walk in before the boys come over? Maybe we could all go? It's gorgeous out there …'

I hadn't really looked, but I was feeling good so it stood to reason that the weather was following my mood.

'... and we could all use a little stretch, don't you think?' I bestowed my most dazzling smile on them, expecting nothing less than agreement.

I shouldn't have been surprised at their collective reaction to my enthusiasm. Apparently they hadn't had the rest that I did, more's the pity, but that didn't stop me from playing Susie Sunshine.

'Oh, c'mon, you guys! We'll just take a quick jaunt around the park, smell a few flowers, then come back and get ready for the day. Whaddya say?' I was not opposed to a wheedle or two if necessary, having honed that particular skill on my brothers. I saw a crack in their united front, Leslie looking at Miss Bea for guidance. For a moment, I saw a flash of LJ there, but it quickly evaporated. In a tone decidedly more Leslie than LJ, she shook her head.

'I'd like to, Jo, really I would, but I'm so tired this morning. I didn't get any sleep to speak of and I just want to take a shower, then rest; maybe read while we wait for LJ and Derek to get here.'

I looked closer at her and saw there were tired lines on her face, and the purple under her eyes was not just a trick of light. I felt ashamed for assuming that everyone had slept as well as I had.

'I second that,' added Miss Lucinda firmly. 'I still need to catch up to the day, I'm that worn out.'

'And I'm not feeling too perky this morning either, my dear.' Miss Bea, bless her heart, looked apologetically at me.

That did it. I was officially censored by the Triad of Tired Women.

'No worries,' I declared briskly. 'I'll take a quick jog around the park, run by and invite the boys over to visit for lunch, and dash home to shower.' I looked at them, feeling an affection for three near-strangers – we really hadn't been together for long – that I didn't have for some of my own flesh and blood, Crazy Great-Aunt Opal notwithstanding.

True to my word, and probably to their collective relief, I took myself out for a walk. The morning air was crisp, with just a hint of the warmth that the day would bring. I found myself taking in deep breaths, incorporating as much of Colorado mountain air as I could into my lungs.

The KOA was quiet this morning, most of the trailers empty of visitors.

Oleta McLaughlin was watering plants outside the office door, and I gave her a brisk wave as I trotted on past. I'd almost reached the boys' trailer when I felt something odd, something that made the hair on the back of my neck stand straight up.

I had spotted Julian Sweet, standing in the shadows near the edge of the campgrounds.

Chapter Twenty-two

I hurried to the door of the boys' trailer, my steps quickened by uneasiness. Or maybe fear. A sleepy-looking LJ pulled open the door, running his hands over hair that seemed to have a life of its own this morning.

'Good morning, LJ,' I said briskly, stepping around him and into the living room. 'Is Derek up yet?'

Still on silent mode, LJ just shook his head. I tell you – conversing with this guy was sometimes akin to that old game 'Charades', where one person mimes the answer.

'OK,' I said slowly, as if the speed of words would make a difference, 'will he be up soon? We want you two to come down for a chat and some lunch, around eleven, all right?'

LJ nodded. Well, at least I had managed to convey the invitation and gotten an RSVP of sorts. I turned to leave.

'Oh, LJ?' An elevated eyebrow from him, indicating that he was listening. 'When I leave, make sure that no one is following me, OK?'

Both eyebrows went skyward at that comment.

With that, I left, glancing quickly at the tree line where I was sure Julian Sweet had been standing. There was nothing there now but shadows of varying darkness.

The return trip to our trailer was a bit swifter than it had been when I first started out, full of morning sunshine and the promise of a better day. I made sure to modify my face before I walked in, knowing that the radar abilities of Miss Bea and Miss Lucinda were nothing short of miraculous.

It didn't work.

As if on a swivel, both sisters-in-law turned their heads toward me and gave me a penetrating, Superman-strength stare as I entered the living room. How did one get that sort of talent, I wondered, as I tried to stroll casually into the kitchen for a glass of water. Nothing doing: they were hot on my tracks.

'OK, OK! I give.' I raised my hands in mock surrender at the two older women, standing shoulder to shoulder – actually, standing shoulder to ribcage because Miss Bea was so short – waiting to hear what I had to say. And I knew they weren't thinking about the boys either.

'I'm pretty sure I saw someone,' I began, not giving the name, out of sheer orneriness.

Miss Lucinda and Miss Bea's eyebrows rose in concert. I sighed.

'I think it was Julian Sweet.' There. I'd given up the information they had come for without much of a battle. I'm telling you: Those two could train the CIA in how to interrogate.

'And what was it about him that's got you all in a twist?' Miss Lucinda, never one for mincing words, spoke first.

'Er, it's just that – well, he was *staring* at me, Miss Lucinda.' Well, *that* sure sounded menacing, I thought. I attempted to explain. 'It was just weird, you know? Here I'd been talking about him with Officer Kingsley, and snap! There he is.'

Miss Bea spoke slowly, head tilted sparrow-style. 'Was he here to visit someone, perhaps? Maybe was on his way to see Derek or LJ?'

That gave me a start. I hadn't even considered that angle. And I didn't like it.

'I hope not! What in the world would he want with them? I mean, we haven't heard squat from him since Josie … since we found Josie, and I can't imagine what he'd need to say to either of them.'

I took a big gulp from my glass of water, managing to spill some down my sweat-soaked T-shirt.

The spilled drink reminded me of Officer Kingsley's own mishap last night, which in turn reminded me of our directive: find a motive for Julian's involvement, if any.

I set the glass down, reaching for a towel to mop up my mess.

Turning toward Miss Bea, I said, 'I think that we should take a closer look at Julian Sweet, I really do. Like I told Officer K last night, the way he just appeared and disappeared the night that Josie was killed – that's too bizarre not to mean something, don't you think?'

Miss Lucinda pursed her lips, thinking. I noticed that a few English muffin crumbs had attached themselves to the corners of her mouth.

'Well, now. That may be worth considering, Jo,' she acquiesced. 'Do you have anything particular in mind?'

I did.

When we had all gathered in the living room following a quick lunch, boys included, I put forward my ideas for the group's consideration. For one thing, as I pointed out, 'it's too obvious for Andy and Skinny Joe to be in on this.'

'True, but remember Joe's odd behavior following Josie's murder,' Derek objected.

'OK, I'll give you that. Especially since I'm the one who brought that particular gem to your attention, Derek. But really,' I continued, 'would you behave like that, if you were the killer?'

'Yes,' he responded promptly. 'I might want to be sure I hadn't left anything behind that could tie me to anything.'

'That's just my point,' I replied. 'That's too obvious a move. I don't think Skinny Joe had anything to do with the killing. I propose we begin with finding out where he was when Lily was killed. Officer Kingsley said that they should have a timeframe for her death sometime this afternoon. I'll give her a call and we'll go from there. Agreed?' I looked around the room at my *compadres*. There were no objections, so on I went.

'The next thing we need to consider is what, if any, motive anyone may have had for either killing. I mean, unless it was really a spur of the moment, mad-passion act, there had to be a reason.'

Leslie raised her hand, exuding 'perfect student'.

I wanted to point to her and say, 'Yes, Leslie?' I kept it to a chin jerk in her direction.

'Have you given any thought to why anyone, say Julian, might want to kill either of those girls? Don't you think that it would have to be someone who knew both of them fairly well?'

I considered that for a moment.

'Yes, I do, but I don't.' Total blank stares from five faces. 'What I mean is this: suppose Josie was killed for what she knew, and then Lily was killed for witnessing it, or telling the killer that she knew he'd done it. Think about the way she was ...'

I couldn't go any further with that thought. Leslie and Derek's faces paled and I found myself swallowing hard.

'Yes, I think I see what you're saying, Jo,' Miss Bea acknowledged. 'It would certainly indicate that maybe Lily had said something that she shouldn't have, perhaps threatened to let the cat out of the bag.'

I nodded. That's what I was trying to say.

'We should be focusing on who would have been afraid Lily might talk, who seemed nervous around her. That's going to be a little tough concerning Julian, especially since he's been virtually invisible since last week.' I looked at Derek and LJ. 'If I remember right, all three of those guys – Andy, Julian, and Bert – worked at some casino around here. You two see if you can find out which one, OK?' They nodded in unison. 'Leslie, you and I can make a few calls, find out how Lily knew Josie, that kind of thing. Come to think of it,' I added, 'Oleta McLaughlin will probably be a good resource.'

Leslie laughed. 'I remember how much information she had on Josie. She'll probably know more about folks around here than people who actually live in Manchester.'

I had to agree. Oleta McLaughlin sounded like a *bona fide* member of the Manchester Gossip Chain.

With Miss Bea and Miss Lucinda holding down the fort, the rest of us dispersed to our assignments. Leslie and I walked down toward the manager's office, enjoying the beautiful day and each other's company. We had become, for lack of a better word, like camp roomies; being with Becklaw's Murder Mystery Tour felt like one long camp adventure.

Except for the two murders, of course. Real camps didn't have anything like that. And movie camps didn't count.

Percy and Oleta were both at home, she bent over a ledger laid out on her desk and he sitting cross-legged on a deep leather chair, reading the paper and whistling under his breath. They both looked up and smiled at us.

'Good morning, good morning!' Oleta's plump face nearly outdid itself in welcome. I thought she was still trying to dispel that first encounter we'd had. She glanced up at a clock. 'Oops. Guess it's actually 'good afternoon',

175

isn't it?'

Percy stood to his feet, long legs unfolding beneath him. 'Can I get you two young ladies coffee? Oleta made a fresh pot not too long ago.'

I briefly wondered what an 'unfresh' pot would taste like, but I kept my answer to a 'Yes, please.'

Armed with cups of coffee strong enough to walk around on their own, Leslie and I chatted about this and that, finally steering the conversation around to Lily and Josie and what might have possibly connected the two. It was like throwing a bone to a starving dog.

Oleta's wealth of local knowledge far surpassed my expectations. She had a solid grasp on who was married to whom, which families had 'issues' – her word – and what made old Mrs Petty down at the grocery store just about come unglued.

'And I do mean that, girls. You should've seen her face! Oh, my – I thought the world was coming to an end.' Oleta paused for breath. That was fortuitous. It gave me time to catch up to her train of thought, which was traveling at light speed on the Manchester Information Railroad.

'So, is there anything that might have made someone upset at the two of them? Something bad enough to get them, you know … killed?' Leslie gulped, her face showing a little of the panic from the day before.

Thankfully, Oleta didn't notice the reticence in Leslie's tone. She was still focused on the delivery of local news and forged ahead.

'Well, I don't know if you'd call it bad enough to get killed over, but I do know that Josie was dating Andy, who's Lily's cousin, and Lily was none too happy about that little arrangement. In fact,' she added with a sly grin, 'I do know that the weekend before last, a bunch of them were at the casino, and something made Andy get so mad at Lily that he wasn't even speaking to her.'

I stared at her. 'What do you mean, Andy was mad at Lily? And how would you know that?' Her participation in the local gossip chain must be more than just 'bearer of news'; she must have achieved 'Captain' status.

'My niece Jess, the one whose husband delivers all the beer to the casinos? Well, she heard from him that Andy and Lily were really going at each other in the parking lot that night. Seems she was furious over something she'd overheard, and I just put two and two together and got Josie.' She smiled triumphantly.

Well. That was certainly a motive, I thought. Maybe we should take a look at dear Andy. I communicated my thoughts to Leslie via telepathy, or at least I tried. She didn't look my way, but I could see her shifting in her seat a bit. Maybe she was thinking along the same lines.

I stood to my feet, draining the last of my very strong coffee and managing to keep my face from screwing up at the bitter taste. Leslie followed suit, and we politely thanked the McLaughlins for their time.

'Any time, my dears, any time. It does get a bit monotonous with just me and Percy.' Oleta gave her husband a fond smile which he didn't see; he had barricaded himself behind the safety of the paper at the first onslaught of gossip.

We walked back to the trailer, me in silence, trying to organize my thoughts, and Leslie gently humming under her breath. I was glad to hear it. She had taken a pretty big blow, emotionally-speaking, yesterday.

We found Miss Bea and Miss Lucinda in the kitchen, working in unison over a large pan of rolled cookies. They were bent over the dough, adding sprinkles of colored sugar and slivered almonds to the tops of the cookies. The entire pan looked as festive as an Easter basket.

'Hello, girls,' smiled Miss Bea. She paused to wipe her

hands on the apron that encompassed her ample waist. 'How did the gossip session go?' Her hair had gone to new heights in frizz, probably from the heat in the kitchen.

I laughed. It was indeed a gossip session *extraordinaire*.

'Really good, Miss Bea. In fact, I think we've got something solid to go on. Have you heard back from the boys yet?'

They had taken the station wagon and driven off to Whispering Stick Hotel and Casino, bent on gathering information on the trio of bit-parters who had joined us in Manchester.

Miss Lucinda, using the back of her dough-covered hand to move some hair out of her face, straightened up, issuing a small groan.

'That Oleta McLaughlin struck me as a bad person to tell a secret to, that's for sure. What'd she tell you girls?'

'Well, she seems to think that something happened to make Lily and Andy fall out, probably over Josie. I'm still trying to work out how that could have led to murder, though.' I sat down in one of the kitchen chairs, stretching my legs out and sighing. Gossip was tiring.

Leslie pulled out the other seat. 'I think,' she said, 'it's possible Lily told Andy something about Josie, maybe that she was dating someone else as well, and he got mad at her for telling and Josie for doing.'

I considered that. It certainly sounded feasible.

'How about this.' Miss Bea carried the finished pan over to the oven and popped it inside, setting the timer. 'What if Andy killed Josie accidentally, and then Lily tried to blackmail him, so he had to kill her as well?'

OK. We were making progress in the motive department, I thought.

'I want to talk to LJ and Derek and see if they were

able to talk to any of the three today,' I said. 'Maybe we should give sleuthing a break for now until they get home.'

The others agreed, and we spent the rest of the afternoon rolling out dough, cutting out cookies in fanciful shapes, and doing a lot of quality assurance tests. Someone had to try them out, didn't they?

Chapter Twenty-three

Eventually we heard the thrum of the station wagon's motor as it pulled next to the trailer. Two doors slammed shut, and two pairs of footsteps made their way up the steps and into the living room.

'We're back!'

I had to grin to myself. Somehow we'd all fallen into a family-like rhythm, retreating into long-ago childhood roles. Well, it suited me. I guess I was missing my own clan more than I cared to admit, and my substitute family helped a lot with homesickness.

'We're in the kitchen,' I called over my shoulder. Derek and LJ walked into the room, sniffing the air like two foraging animals.

'Umm! What smells so good?' Derek asked as he rescued two iced cookies that threaten to topple from the tall pile in the center of the table.

'Me,' I said saucily, tossing a cookie at LJ, who caught it in his massive hands.

'Oh, hardee har har, Jo,' returned Derek, his words muffled in a huge swallow.

'How was the hunt, boys?' inquired Miss Lucinda, expertly stacking more cookies on the pile. 'Learn anything good?'

'Maybe.' Derek took another large bite of cookie,

dropping crumbs down the front of his shirt. He licked one finger and swiped at them, earning an eye roll from me.

Boys, I thought. You just can't take them anywhere.

The four of us – and LJ – gave him our full attention. What I got out of his spiel was this:

Andy and Bert had been good friends from kindergarten straight through to high school, and Julian joined them in their junior year at Manchester High. Andy and Bert's lives were pretty much an open book in the area, having been born and bred there. Not much was known about Julian's background, other than that his dad wasn't in the picture and his mother had passed away two years before. The trio had worked together at the casino for the past three years, and recently most folks had noticed that Julian had been keeping to himself. Other than that, the three guys seemed to be fairly normal, not the murdering kind.

We sat silent, digesting both the information and the cookies. I glanced at the plate. At the rate they were disappearing, none of us were going to have much appetite for real food this evening.

'OK.' I said. 'I've got a great idea, everyone. How about a Becklaw group visit to Whispering Stick Hotel and Casino for an evening of fun? And, hopefully, get more info on Andy.' I looked around the kitchen. 'Well?'

'I'm up for it,' spoke up Miss Lucinda. 'And I heard they've got an awesome buffet up there, too.'

Trust Miss Lucinda to bring food into it. That woman could out-eat anyone.

No one else said anything, so I smiled brightly at Miss Lucinda and said, 'Sounds like we've got a date. What time should we leave?'

'I think I want to go, too,' Leslie spoke up. LJ nodded as well, no surprise there. Derek shrugged but nodded. He was in.

Miss Bea sighed. 'I really don't like casinos,' she said. 'But I'm not staying home alone. So I guess I'll go too. Let's leave around five-thirty.'

I'm always a sucker for a field trip. Remember those visits to the local zoo or museum when you were a kid and every day was an adventure? That's exactly how I was feeling as I went to my room to lie down for a bit. I had a sixth sense that something would turn up this evening that would point us in the right direction.

We loaded up the wagon promptly at five-thirty, ready to party and eat buffet until we popped. Derek drove, telling us about the casino's layout, the different areas for gaming, and the large poker room.

'You're gonna love it, Miss Bea,' he said over his shoulder. 'It's got one room that's decorated in nothing but old movie star posters.' I sincerely hoped that this was a nod to her tastes and not to her age.

We pulled up into a spacious parking lot that was more than halfway filled with vehicles of every description, from fancy sedans to trucks sporting campers, the windows plastered with hunting decals. Derek slotted the station wagon between a Volkswagen Beetle, adorned with a bumper sticker that read 'My other car is a sewing machine', and a low-slung Mini Cooper, its exterior a shiny red. Next to them, the station wagon looked like a lumbering beast.

With Derek and LJ leading the way, we paraded into the main lobby of the casino.

It was amazing. The ceiling rose to a peak above us in a cathedral-like design, chandeliers hanging like so many twinkling stars far above our heads. The walls were just as impressive, covered in murals depicting the majesty of the Colorado landscape. Here and there among the painted trees, I spotted eyes staring out at me. I shuddered. I didn't think that I'd ever feel the same about animals again, especially not those in the small category.

After a few minutes of tourist-like gaping we made our way to the buffet area. A strong aroma of garlic met us at the door, assuring us that 'Italian Night' was in full swing. Winding our way over to the line, we each grabbed a tray and got ready to plow through the many choices. I stood between Miss Bea and Derek, she looking eagerly over my shoulder and he already taking a roll from the basket that sat nearest the silverware caddies. Well. This would be a gastronomical adventure. And I was ready to meet the challenge.

Two plates, three desserts, and one very large glass of iced tea later, I succumbed. Further down the table, I saw Miss Lucinda, she of the cast-iron stomach, also in a state of surrender, rummaging through her voluminous purse. She was probably looking for antacid tablets.

I was right. She was popping the chalky pink tabs like after-dinner mints.

Finally dinner was over, at least for the Becklaw bunch. We staggered to our collective feet and retraced our, steps out to the main lobby. I had retained leader status, *à la* Miss Jo of the Wild West, and I made an executive decision: we would go in pairs and look for Bert, Andy, and Julian. I teamed up with Miss Lucinda, and we set off, our eyes peeled for Andy.

I had an idea that he would be among the gaming tables somewhere, recalling that Skinny Joe had mentioned something about dealing cards. With Miss Lucinda looking right and me looking left, we casually circled the casino floor, our tourist faces firmly in place. I finally spotted him near the back of the room, running the roulette table.

He kept up a stream of professional patter with the folks gathered around the wheel, keeping them loose enough to throw more chips on the table. I had to admire his easy manner; he wasn't uptight, like someone who had just committed two murders should be.

As he leaned over to give the wheel a spin, I caught his eye and waggled my fingers at him. He managed to control his facial expression, but I could see the muscles around his jaw tighten. He was not happy to see me.

We waited until the current game was over and sauntered to the table, slipping onto a pair of high-backed stools. Andy continued to fiddle with the wheel, acting as though we weren't there.

'Hiya, Andy,' I said brightly. 'It's a lovely evening. And I simply adore what they've done to this place! So cosmopolitan, you know?' I was getting to him.

He glared at me, giving me a once-over that was not in the least bit friendly. Or flattering.

'What? I'm busy here, in case you didn't notice.' His words were clipped off as clean as a knife's edge, and I forced myself to hold his gaze.

'Why, we just wanted to take a look at your casino, being visitors to the area and all,' I returned, ramping up the wattage of my smile. 'And to have a wee chat, if you don't mind.'

'I do mind; now scram before I call Security.' He stood to his feet, scanning the room as though looking for backup.

'Sit down, young man,' barked Miss Lucinda in her best school teacher voice. Andy sat. I really need to perfect that tone.

Without much persuasion, Andy began to tell us what we wanted know: yes, he had dated Josie – exclusively, he'd thought, until Lily had opened her trap. No, he did not get mad enough to kill either one of them. He had no idea who would have, either.

'The only time the two of them were together, beside the acting thing, was when we all came here to the casino on '80s Night.'

'Who's "we"?' I asked, that familiar feeling starting to creep up my spine.

'Well, there was me, and Josie. Bert and Lily. Julian was there, and someone else who's name I don't recall. That's about it.' He looked at me. 'Now if that's it, I need to get back to work. My boss keeps looking over here.'

I had a feeling that there was more, something he knew. Maybe even something he didn't even realize he knew. I stalled, hoping to come up with the right question.

'What were you all talking about?' I asked, noting the incoming pit boss off to my right. We had to hurry.

'Just about the robbery.' Andy sounded casual, but he had seen his boss's approach as well. He started fiddling with the cards.

'What robbery?' This was something, all right.

'Well, not really a robbery, as such – just that someone had been skimming money out of the night deposits. We were teasing each other, and Julian was getting huffy.'

The pit boss, a large man sporting a handlebar moustache and a ring on every finger, stood silently over Andy, arms folded and a frown on his face.

'Good evening, Marc,' Andy said. 'They were just leaving.'

We got up and moved off, my mind still on Andy's last words. Julian had gotten mad over the teasing. In my experience with all of my brothers, the one who got the angriest was the one who had something to hide.

Julian had gotten mad. Now we were heading someplace.

We met as planned by the front door. I was quiet, turning a few ideas over in my head. The others were chatting about the games and the clients, exclaiming over the old man who had hit the double jackpot on a nickel slot machine. In his excitement, at least twenty dollars' worth of shiny five cent pieces had bounced on the floor at his feet, giving him the appearance of sinking in silver quicksand. Apparently, only Andy had been scheduled to work this night, so no joy with contacting Bert or Julian. The other four weren't complaining; they'd had a blast.

With Derek piloting us home, we arrived at the KOA just after eleven o'clock. I was tired. Miss Bea had already nodded off, and even LJ's massive head drooped a bit. I knew that I wouldn't be able to sleep, though, not right away. Too many scenarios were playing out in my mind, with Julian Sweet in the leading role.

Well, when in a quandary, look to Crazy Great-Aunt Opal for advice. The gem I came up with this time was this: "A good question is half the answer."

My problem was articulating the question.

Chapter Twenty-four

In spite of my worries over a good night's sleep, I did OK. To be honest, I was more anxious over what the next day would bring, i.e. Julian Sweet, and working out what made him so angry at Andy and Company. I wasn't looking forward to talking to him, but that was the only way I figured we could get at the truth.

I kept seeing him in my mind's eye, standing at the edge of the trees, in the shadows. It was as if he wanted me to see him. Wanted me to notice him. Not to worry, Julian, I thought grimly. I saw you.

Breakfast was a little subdued. The old dears had stayed out a little later than they were used to, and this morning they were feeling the after-effects. And bless their dear hearts, they still got up at the regular time, putting the toast in the toaster and tea on the table. Miss Bea's hair was at its best– or worst, depending on your view– this morning, the frizzy mess piled high over one ear and anchored there with a maze of hairpins. Not to be outdone by her sis-in-law, Miss Lucinda's lavender mop was arranged in a massive bun at the back of her head, two pencils stuck through it at odd angles to keep it there. I shook my head in amusement; if I lived to be their age, I could only hope to have the same panache.

Finally full, I stood up and began clearing the table, stacking our crumb-covered plates and teacups carefully.

Leslie followed suit, carrying the empty teapot and butter over to the counter. Miss Bea and Miss Lucinda stood up and walked to the front room, still in the process of waking up. I had noticed before that when Miss Lucinda was extremely tired, she tended to limp a bit more than usual. This morning, the limp was pronounced.

While Leslie washed the dishes, I rinsed and dried. We worked well together; maybe the two of us should work on Julian today and leave the Becklaw women behind to rest. I put the idea to Leslie, who promptly agreed.

We got ready in record time. I recalled the adage that had come to me the night before, the one about the question being half of the answer. I needed to frame the question in such a way that I got the answer I needed. How to do that was still the issue.

On the drive into town, I hit up Leslie with a plan. 'Let's go by Julian's house.'

She looked sideways at me as she drove, one eyebrow hiked up. 'And?'

'Well, I don't know. It'll come to us when we get there.' I looked out of the passenger window at the landscape that was becoming as familiar to me as that of my home in Piney Woods.

'Jo, we need a reason for stopping by his place. We can't just waltz up to his door and ask if he's the killer.'

She had a point.

'OK, then. What should we say?' I must admit I hadn't one decent idea in mind. The only thing I could think of was trying to make that elusive connection between getting mad at some buddies over being teased and the deaths of two young women. That was certainly a stretch.

'Oh, I don't know. Maybe tell him what you learned from Andy, then just see how he reacts.' Leslie signaled a left turn, and we pulled into our usual spot behind the library.

First things first, though. We needed to use the library's phone directory collection to ferret out Julian's address. It was still a bit early, only eight-forty, and the library opened at nine. I suggested a short constitutional around downtown Manchester.

We locked up the station wagon, Leslie shoving the keys deep into her jeans pocket. Setting off toward the center of town, we began to stroll, enjoying the morning. Colorado in the spring, even high in the mountains, can be deceptive. A day can begin as gray and dismal as a dungeon, only for the clouds to break apart and the sun to shine in full glory. On the other hand, a sunny morning did not guarantee a sunny afternoon, so I had learned to take advantage of days like this.

We had just passed the post office and were approaching the craft shop when Leslie grabbed at my arm. 'Don't look!' she hissed.

Of course I looked. And I saw him, leaning against the corner of the store across the street, sipping a coffee and watching us, not bothering to hide that he was staring.

Julian Sweet, slightly built and not in the least physically intimidating, made my skin crawl. I had not one reason why, I couldn't even begin to explain. I just had That Feeling again. Locking eyes with me, Julian made sure that I saw him, then casually turned and walked back the other way, tossing his cup into a trash can.

I fished my cellphone out of my pocket, noticing I had three missed calls, all the same number. I groaned. Mother again. I'd really have to make an effort.

'I'm going to give Officer Kingsley a call,' I told Leslie, thumbing through the contacts list until I located her number, then pressed the little green telephone icon to place the call.

'Kingsley,' came the abrupt answer. She certainly

didn't waste any breath on unnecessary words, I'd noticed.

'Good morning, it's Jo Anderson calling.' I waited for her to acknowledge me and got only an earful of dead air. 'Hello?'

'I'm here. How can I help?' Officer K sounded a bit grumpy this bright Colorado morning, so I came to the point quickly.

'Can we – Leslie and I – come by and talk to you? We're in town right now …' I broke off as she interrupted me.

'Look. I appreciate your concern, I really do. But I'm up to my eyeballs in these murders, along with the nonsense up at the casino last night, so now's not exactly a good time to see you.'

'We were at the casino last night,' I offered. 'I didn't notice any nonsense going on, only that crazy drunk lady who kept falling all over the place.'

The silence this time was attentive. I could hear papers rustling as Officer Kingsley moved things about. 'Could you two swing by the office in about ten minutes? I'm on my way to a quick meeting, but I can meet you in the lobby at nine.'

I calculated quickly. We could just make it there if we hoofed it right now. I know we had the car, but I wanted to walk off some of my renewed energy, maybe get a spark of something fired up in my brain. 'We'll be there,' I promised, then disconnected.

'What's that all about?' asked Leslie as we turned around and began walking in the direction of the police station.

'I'm not sure. Something about the casino. I told her we were there last night, and now she wants to see us.'

We made it there in record time, only slightly out of breath. The officer at the front desk told us to wait, that

Officer Kingsley would be down in a minute. We plopped down into a pair of chairs. The lobby was typical of your average police station, not, I hasten to add, that I've spent much time in one. The line-up of plastic chairs, the kind that stick to the backs of sweaty legs, the 'Most Wanted' posters around the walls, the metal detectors by all doors, both in and out. A most depressing place, I thought.

The near door swung open and Officer Kingsley stood there, one ear covered with her cellphone. She motioned for us to follow her back, giving the desk sergeant a brief wave. We followed her through the warren of offices, some occupied, others dark and silent. This time she took us to her office, shutting the door behind us before moving around to the other side of her desk and sitting down.

She was still listening intently to whoever it was on the other end of the line, so Leslie and I amused ourselves by studying the many commendations hung around the room. Apparently Officer K was well-liked and successful at her job.

Finally the call ended, and after a brief moment to look over the notes she had been taking, Officer Kingsley looked up at us, a serious expression on her face.

'OK. Tell me what you know about the casino.'

Leslie and I looked at each other, completely baffled. What in the world was she talking about?

'Could you maybe give us a hint? I mean, we were there last night, sure, but nothing happened.' Unless that creepy pit boss had reported me and Miss Lucinda as stalkers. That was always a possibility, I admitted.

'After the last deposit was made, the night office was broken into and most of the money was taken. I say 'most' because some of it was still in the bag when we were called out early this morning.'

I took a good look at Officer Kingsley. She did indeed have the appearance of one not getting a proper amount of rest.

I considered my words, then offered, 'Andy Grimes, one of the extras that Miss Bea had hired to play in our performance, told me that he thought Julian Sweet had a weird reaction when some of the other employees teased him about being the burglar.' OK, not technically true. But still, if I could have gotten Andy to talk more, he *might* have said that.

Officer Kingsley stared at me a moment then pulled her notebook closer to her and readied her pen. 'OK. Tell me what you know, Jo.'

I spent the next few minutes recapping the conversation with Andy, how I felt that somehow the murders were tied up with the burglaries – never mind that I couldn't articulate it – and that Julian, again, was the center of the issue.

To her credit, Officer K took me seriously, or appeared to, and for that I was grateful. I'd had my fill of being the 'special' member of the group, the one whose actions and reactions were considered borderline nutcase at best.

'Let me pass this on to the others on my team. I'll give you a call if I need to talk to you again, OK?' She stood to her feet, indicating the meeting was at an end.

Leslie and I took our time strolling back toward the library. I had a sudden urge for a bagel and cream cheese, and I knew that the small grocery store on the next block boasted a deli/bakery combo.

And I recalled Oleta McLaughlin's comments about someone who worked there who had talked about Josie. Maybe this fount of knowledge would also want to talk about Julian Sweet.

Chapter Twenty-five

The store's interior was dim compared to the outdoors. Glancing up at the ceiling, I figured it out for myself: half the lights were turned off; probably their nod to the Green Movement.

The deli and bakery shared an area near the back of the store, and that's where we headed. The bagel and cream cheese craving had grown to include a crème horn and an iced sugar cookie. I blamed it on the fresh mountain air.

While we waited our turn, Leslie and I perused the offerings inside the bakery's glass cabinets. Trays of glazed donuts, some iced and covered in sprinkles, sat beside huge apple fritters, puffed and warm and ready to melt in your mouth. Cookies of all kinds, croissants and bagels – it was all here.

'Can I help you?' The pleasant-looking young girl behind the counter smiled at us, plastic gloves at the ready.

I gave her our order and we watched as she retrieved the goodies and popped them inside a waxed paper bag emblazoned with the store's name and logo. We paid for our purchases and were just walking away when someone from behind the deli side of things called out, 'Ain't you girls part of that traveling show? The one where that girl got killed?'

Swell. Just what I needed – not! I'd made up my mind

to ignore the joker and walk out, when Leslie stopped beside me, turning toward the voice.

'If you are speaking of Becklaw's Murder Mystery Tour that got canceled due to a murder then yes, that's us. Can I help you with something?' Leslie's voice was polite, that dangerous form of acquiescence that indicates temper. Ms Deli Counter had better be careful, I thought.

'I was talking to Aunt Oleta about you the other day. That Josie, she was one bad girl. Always messing with others' boyfriends, starting trouble with gossip,'– as if what she was doing wasn't gossip –'and making life miserable in general around here. Can't say I'm sorry she's gone.'

By this time we had edged nearer to the tall counter holding meats and cheeses, close enough to see the gal that stood on the opposite side of the glass, a stained apron tied around a middle that mimicked her Aunt Oleta's to a tee. Not all family traits were winners.

'I'm sorry you feel that way about Josie, er ... Lola,' I said, reading her name from the badge riding on her ample chest. Hmm. Another reminder of her familial ties.

Lola snorted. 'You have no idea, missy,' she said defensively. 'Why, she nearly wrecked my own house with her giggling and swaying and carrying on. Every man in town just about lost their eyeballs starin' at her.' Lola slammed a half ham down on the slicing counter as if she had Josie in her hands.

I looked at Leslie from the corner of my eye. Now here was yet another motive being bandied about: the spurned woman angle. From where I stood, things were getting crazier and more confusing.

Leslie had started inching back toward me, my cue to say brightly, 'Oh, would you look at the time! Leslie, we need to get back. Nice talking to you, Lola.'

We made our escape, bakery bag clutched tightly in my

hand. I wasn't about to lose seven dollars and twenty-two cents' worth of sweets.

Once on the comparatively safe street, I turned to Leslie, asking, 'What was *that* all about?'

She shrugged. 'I thought that maybe she'd give us something else to work with. Instead, she came off as the Crazed Wife of Manchester.'

I agreed. Lola and her Aunt Oleta were indeed cut from the same cloth.

In tacit agreement, we made our way back to the library. It was open now, but I sat down on a bench near the entrance, face to the sunshine and hand in the bakery bag. I needed a sugar hit before I tackled another person involved in these crimes. Leslie and I munched in silent contentment, recharging our mental batteries and thinking about the next step: getting Julian's address and paying him a visit.

Goodies eaten, address obtained, we made our way back to the station wagon. And froze. Wedged under one wiper blade was what looked like a wadded up paper napkin. We inched toward it cautiously, not knowing what to expect.

'Shouldn't you call Officer Kingsley?' Leslie, asked me, sounding a tad nervous. I laughed. 'What for? Because someone stuck their trash on Miss Bea's car?' I reached out to free the object, then snatched my hand back. Something was moving inside the wad of paper.

I looked on the ground for a stick or something to poke with, and spied the broken end of someone's car antenna lying near the back tire. I picked it up and stopped, the antenna frozen skyward in my hand like a – well, like an antenna.

It was Miss Bea's. Whoever had stuck that little gift under the wiper blade had also taken the opportunity to let us know that this wasn't a joke. OK – it was time to call

Officer Kingsley.

We waited for the cavalry to arrive, huddled together on the bench beside the library. Within a few minutes, we saw the familiar black and white come pulling up to the curb, Officer K emerging from the passenger's door. She and her partner, a short burly man with arms as big around as my thighs, walked over to meet us. I saw them glance at the car before coming over, but they made no comment. Maybe cops have their own telepathic communication.

I had used the past few minutes to take stock of my life as it had transpired up until now. I had to conclude that no one in their right mind would have ever put me in the middle of anything like this. All I had wanted to do was to see the world and get out from underneath my mother's thumb and watchful eye.

Actually, that seemed like a fairly safe place to be right then.

'Jo? Leslie? You two OK?' Officer Kingsley stopped in front of us, her back to the sun.

I had to cover my eyes as I tried to look her in the face, but the slanted rays of the morning light were too strong. I stood.

'I'm OK, thanks, just a little upset. Not as upset as Miss Bea's going to be, though,' I added, handing her the busted antenna.

Leslie nodded. 'We were in the library for about ten minutes and the car was perfectly fine when we went in, wasn't it, Jo?'

She turned to me for confirmation and I nodded. Nothing untoward had jumped out at me as we had walked by. Of course, I had been focusing on the goodies from the bakery.

As if she could read my thoughts, Officer Kingsley looked at me, her eyebrows lifted in question. I blushed.

'Well, maybe I was in a hurry to get at the bagels and cookies we just bought,' I confessed. 'I really didn't look *at* the car, but I think that I would have noticed something.'

Officer K's expression clearly said, maybe, maybe not. One thing for sure: I was getting much better at reading others' faces.

'Let's take a look at the windshield, shall we?' The two officers walked over to the station wagon's front end, snapping on gloves as they walked. This looked semi-serious, and my heart began to pick up the pace.

The brawny officer leaned in closer, poking at the object with the end of one gloved finger. I saw something moving again, then the tip of a long tail – a long, skinny tail, to be exact – emerged. Cupping both hands around the wriggling mass, he turned around to face us, showing us the tiny mouse that had been tied to the stick that ran along its back, the stick then thrust through the paper. Poor thing. It must have been in shock.

I must be in shock! I was feeling sorry for a mouse!

We made it through the interview process, our plans to visit Julian's house shelved for the present. I say 'the present' because I was still working from feelings I had about him and his connection to Josie and Lily. There was definitely something there, something tenuous, but there nonetheless. With the assurance that this was some mindless prank– nothing had been written on the paper, after all – we took off.

After that little escapade, we decided to go on back to the campground. I hadn't called anyone and told them about our predicament, deciding it would be better to tell Miss Bea in person about her beloved station wagon.

The KOA was bustling with new visitors. The McLaughlins were standing outside talking to some new folks, a young couple with a child that seemed to be hopped up on sugar or something. The little girl's stubby pigtails bounced as she jumped frenetically from boulder to decorative boulder, her parents oblivious and Mrs McLaughlin barely able to contain herself. I grinned. Better her than me.

Leslie parked the vehicle in its accustomed spot beside our trailer and killed the motor. We had barely stepped out of the car when the door flew open, two anxious faces peering out at us.

Miss Bea and Miss Lucinda looked upset, and I wondered if maybe Officer Kingsley had called after all to tell them about the damage to her station wagon. I steeled myself for an explanation.

'Oh, Jo! Leslie! I'm so glad you're back! We didn't know what to do, did we, Lucinda?' Miss Bea turned to look up into Miss Lucinda's eyes, who shook her head.

'What's wrong?' Leslie asked in concern as we walked up the steps into the living room. I gave the room a cursory once-over; everything seemed to be in one piece.

'That young man, the one who was going to be in the performance – oh, what was his name, Beatrice? – he came by about thirty minutes ago and asked us to give this to you girls.' Here, Miss Lucinda held out an envelope.

I took it gingerly, holding it by the corner in case it too held a mouse or some other critter. 'Bert. That's who it was, Lucinda.' Miss Bea looked at me. 'He seemed anxious that you have this right away and we couldn't remember your cellphone numbers, could we, Lucinda?'

I relaxed. Their anxiety was over not having our numbers handy, which, now that I thought of it, was not a smart thing for us to have let happen. We needed to post our contact information where everyone could see it.

Slipping my forefinger under the edge of the sealed envelope, I opened it and pulled out a single folded sheet. I read it, my eyes opening wide and my mouth joining suit.

Without a word, I handed it over to Leslie, who had been trying to read over my shoulder.

'We thought you'd be interested in knowing that Julian Sweet has a gambling debt of over 40,000 dollars.' She read the note aloud, and I saw Miss Bea and Miss Lucinda's expressions move from anxiety to disbelief to something akin to anger.

'Would someone please tell me what a person like that is doing working at a casino?' demanded Miss Lucinda, arms akimbo. 'That's like have an alcoholic for a bartender, which, now that I think about it, most of them probably are.'

'Oh, come now, Lucy,' soothed Miss Bea. 'You can't save the world, you know.'

'I can sure give it a try,' declared her sister-in-law. I believed her.

Chapter Twenty-six

Over a late lunch of beef tips on toast– our supplies were running low and we had to get inventive with our meals – we talked about the connection between Julian's gambling problems and two murders.

I voted on Josie being his bookie runner or whatever they were called, while Leslie suggested that perhaps Josie had overheard something she shouldn't have and was taunting Julian with the information. Between the two suppositions, Leslie's made more sense. Recalling what little I had known of her, I couldn't see Josie as a go-between for anyone; she liked the spotlight too much.

The boys showed up just as dessert was put on the table. In this department we were still doing fine. I had whipped together one of my favorites: Extra Easy Fudge, requiring only three ingredients. It had the capability to wipe out the most obnoxious sweet tooth and made men putty in my hands. I know – I had tried it on my brothers often enough.

Once the table had been cleared and we had settled in with mugs of Miss Bea's strong coffee, the work began in earnest. Leslie and I recapped our day's adventure, the contents of the note from Bert and Andy, and the way we thought Julian fitted in with all of this.

'Not to mention we saw him skulking,'– not *skulking*, interrupted Leslie, just *staring* – 'when we were in town this morning.' Whatever you called it, it was downright creepy in my book. I turned to Miss Lucinda. 'Would you say that Bert seemed nervous when he came by?'

She thought, then said slowly, 'No, not nervous like you'd normally think of nervous. Just a bit on edge. Wouldn't you agree, Beatrice?'

Miss Bea nodded in confirmation, her patented frizz bobbing in time to the movement.

'Definitely on edge, Jo. In fact, I thought he had come with someone, the way he kept looking over his shoulder.'

Hmm. That was interesting. Maybe he was on the lookout for Julian Sweet as well, I surmised.

'The good news is that Officer Kingsley thinks that the mouse package was all a prank. The bad part is that I don't. When you put everything together that happened today, beginning with Julian's weird behavior, I'd have to say it all ties in.' I looked around at my fellow troupers, who were listening soberly.

Finally Derek spoke up. 'Look, Jo. If Julian is the main suspect in all of this, why hasn't he been arrested?'

Point taken. I had wondered that myself. All I could think of was that nothing could be tied to Julian, or that they were keeping tabs on him, ready to spring when he did something else. What that 'something else' might be I didn't want to contemplate.

'I haven't a clue, Derek. But I'm all for tracking him down ourselves. I know that Officer Kingsley asked for help with motive – although now I think that was just a ploy to get me out of her hair – and I think we've got it. When you owe as much money as he does and income doesn't equal outgoings, something's got to give. I vote for another trip to the casino.'

Derek's eyes lit up; I could tell he was hearing the dings and noises of the slot machines.

'To gather information, not money,' I added drily.

'Actually,' Leslie said, 'I thought about dinner out at the restaurant we all like so much. It's evening time, which is prime information-gathering time in Manchester, according to my sources.' She smiled enigmatically.

Her sources? *What* sources? I looked at her, trying to retrieve information via a mind-meld, Anderson-style.

Miss Lucinda snorted, but it was a nice sort of noise. In fact, I think that it could have passed for a chuckle; one could never be sure with Miss Lucinda.

'Sounds good, Leslie. I don't think that I could take another meal of beef-on-bread or whatever the heck it was we ate.' She shot Miss Bea a look that said *I dare you to disagree.*

Thankfully, Miss Bea got the message loud and clear. Dinner in town it would be. I was ready to tackle that menu again.

Right on seven o'clock, due to our late lunchtime, we piled into the vehicle, *sans* antenna, and headed off for Manchester's night life. The restaurant's small lot was full and we had to park along the street, something that Leslie and I weren't too keen on, considering our earlier experience.

To my surprise, Lola, Oleta McLaughlin's opinionated niece, was there, playing hostess and seating folks. She grinned when she spotted me. 'My in-laws own this joint. We all have to take turns in the free labor department.' She glanced over her shoulder as if looking for said in-laws.

I was delighted to see her, actually. Here was one person primed for gossip already.

We were finally seated near the back of the restaurant at a round table set up 'family style', a revolving Lazy Susan in the middle filled with salt and pepper, napkins, Tabasco sauce, and the like. Derek gave it an experimental twirl, knocking the salt onto the table.

Quick as a flash, LJ reached down and righted the shaker, pinching up a bit and tossing it over his left shoulder – and directly into the unsuspecting eyes of the rather large man behind us. With a yelp that could raise the roof, he leapt to his feet and began what I'd call a 'jig', howling and clutching at his reddening face.

LJ just sat as if nothing had happened, enigmatic as always. Leslie was horrified, unable to do anything except watch the spectacle. Derek was grinning, and I'm afraid I was amused as well. The man was acting like he'd been pepper sprayed or something.

Lola had rushed over by this time, a wet towel in hand which she pressed against the man's face. Somehow she got him calmed down, promised a 'comp' meal, and left for her post near the front door.

With order restored, we resumed our perusal of the menu. At our last meal here, I had wavered between the shrimp skewers on rice pilaf and the pulled pork hero sandwich. By the time our waitress reappeared, standing out of range of LJ, I noticed, I had settled on the Chicken Fajita Pita platter. I know, I know. I am a woman of fickle tastes, but it makes for an interesting life.

With food in our bellies and a renewed sense of energy, we paid and left the restaurant. While I can't say that we actually got any more gossipy tips that evening, we did have a good time together, family-style.

A stroll around the town was out due to darkness, but walking around the well-lit campground sounded good to all except Miss Lucinda. Her 'poor leg', as she called it, was paining her and she needed to get off it for a while. So, after depositing her in a chair with a book, cellphone, and the promise to be gone 'just a bit', we left for a breath of air, Miss Bea's short legs working hard to keep up with the rest of us.

I was beginning to love Colorado, and the Colorado springtime weather in particular. Crisp air and bright blue skies gave it the feel of being on the top of the world, untouched by pollution and contamination. The McLaughlins had done a great job with the park's layout, and there were several clearly marked trails around and through the KOA. That night we took the longest trail, which led down to the driveway and back around the camp's perimeter. There were soft electric lights every so many feet, but the darkness edged in, throwing shadows from behind every trailer and tree we passed.

We had just started on the last leg of the trek when that familiar tingle attacked my spine, working its way from the nape of my neck downward. I reached for Derek's arm and gave it a quick tug, motioning to him to walk beside me.

'I'm having one of my 'feelings' again,' I murmured. He looked at me, one eyebrow cocked.

I had stopped walking, scanning the area around us and to our immediate right where the forest grew up to meet the KOA boundaries. There was the lightest movement in the trees, too loud for wind and too measured for an animal. Derek heard it as well, and he casually reached down and raked up a handful of forest detritus, pebbles and all. The other three had continued on, chattering among themselves, unaware we had even stopped.

I gave Derek a slight nod and suddenly he turned to face the tree line, launching the rocks and dirt clutched in his hand. It must have found its target, and the result sounded much like the salt incident in the restaurant. Whoever was out there had just become the recipient of a face full of dirt.

With much crashing of branches, the mystery stalker took off, heading deeper into the woods.

I let him go, and Derek showed no inclination for

charging into the darkness. Message delivered and received, I smiled grimly. If it was Julian Sweet, then he knew we were on to him and ready.

All the chaos had alerted Miss Bea, Leslie, and LJ and they came scrambling back, Miss Bea clucking like a mother hen protecting her chicks.

'What in heaven's name, Jo?' she asked, looking from me to Derek, then down at his dirt-encrusted hand. Her eyebrows rose so high they nearly reached her hairline. I answered for him.

'We had a visitor, Miss Bea,' I explained. 'Derek gave him – or her – LJ's 'salt treatment …' – here LJ blushed – '… and whoever it was took off.'

'Salt treatment'?' Miss Bea sounded baffled, and I hastened to enlighten her.

'You know. The old 'salt in the eyes' routine? Only we didn't have salt. Derek threw dirt.'

I smiled at him. He had done well.

'Well. That's good. I guess,' Miss Bea said, sounded a trifle doubtful. 'Are you sure it was a person and not some innocent animal?'

Yes. I was certain. 'I had a feeling, Miss Bea,' I replied. The others, to their credit, did not look askance at me. Instead, they seemed to understand what I meant.

Progress at last.

We continued back to the trailer at a faster pace than we had at the beginning. Miss Lucinda was by herself and I was feeling a bit nervous. The lights were on when we got back and the front door was still locked, yet something felt a bit off.

We sent LJ in first, brave people that we were, and he stood in the middle of the living room, glancing around. Miss Lucinda was nowhere to be seen.

Chapter Twenty-seven

Now was not the time to panic, I admonished myself. I pushed past LJ and headed toward the kitchen. Maybe she was making a snack.

'Miss Lucinda? Are you here?' I called out, trying to keep my voice soft so as not to raise the level of alarm.

There was no answer. I looked back over my shoulder to where the other four stood, huddled together like birds on a telephone wire. I shook my head.

'Leslie, can you go check her room? She might have gone for a lie down, although by now we should've woken her,' I said.

We waited silently until Leslie called out a negative. OK. Maybe she had gone to join us on the walk in spite of her leg pain.

'Derek, can you and LJ retrace our steps around the campground? She may have followed us and had to stop and rest.' I felt like an army general, but no one else was moving.

'We women will stay here in case she shows up, OK?'

Off the boys went, starting in the direction opposite to the beginning of our walk. Miss Bea stayed in the doorway of the kitchen, hands clasped in front of her and eyes closed. Leslie met my eyes and waggled her cellphone at me. I could have slapped my forehead. Miss Lucinda had a cell with her.

I nodded to Leslie, who slipped into the living room to make her call. I could hear her murmuring, waiting a moment and then chuckling. What in the world was so amusing about losing an old woman?

I waited until she came back in to the kitchen to question her, but when I saw her face, I knew everything was OK.

'That Miss Lucinda! She took it on herself to go information gathering and she figured that Oleta McLaughlin was as good a place as any to begin. She's there having coffee and a good gossip.' Leslie shook her head in fond amusement.

This bit of news didn't do anything for Miss Bea, though; if anything, her fear morphed into something like anger. Oops! If I were Miss Lucinda, I wouldn't plan on quality sleep this night.

With this little problem out of the way, we could refocus on the issue of the person who was spying on us during our walk.

Derek and LJ returned and we filled them in on Miss Lucinda's visit to the McLaughlins, adding that I thought they should go escort her back to the trailer just to be on the safe side. The next thing was to consider our plans for the following day, all the more important now.

Once we were all back together, Miss Lucinda included, and not quite meeting Miss Bea's eyes, we laid out the order for the next day. It was clear to all of us that Julian was either a) the killer or b) connected to the murders in some fashion. With that firmly set, we decided that Derek, Miss Bea, Leslie, and I would go into town for an audience with Officer Kingsley, while Miss Lucinda and LJ would hold down the fort here. (I also felt that Miss Lucinda needed a babysitter at this point, plus I didn't think she needed to be traipsing all over town with her bad leg.)

With 'goodnights' exchanged and the boys headed off to their own beds, we gals reconvened in the kitchen, Miss Bea careful not to sit next to Miss Lucinda. I grinned as I caught Leslie's eye; these women could hold a grudge longer than anyone I knew. Be that as it may, I still wanted to hear what Miss Lucinda had gleaned from Oleta McLaughlin.

'So?' I looked at Miss Lucinda, one eyebrow cocked in query.

'Well,' she began. 'That woman really has an issue with Josie. I'm beginning to think that there is more history there than we know about.'

I thought back to the first time we talked to Lola, Oleta's niece. She was adamant that Josie's demise was linked to the cavalier way she acted with other women's men. With that in mind, I asked,

'Did Mrs McLaughlin say anything at all about Lola and Josie? I mean, about Lola's husband and Josie?'

Miss Lucinda thought for a moment then slowly nodded her head. 'Yes, she did. I didn't think much of it then, but you might be on to something here, Jo.'

I almost ground my teeth; I hate conversations where I have to tease information out of folks like a dentist pulling teeth. 'And?'

'Well, there was a to-do at the restaurant – you know, the one we like so much? Apparently Josie had come in there one evening looking for Hap, Lola's hubby. Lola happened to be there as well, and it was all on.'

'Like a fist fight on? That kind?' I was amazed. How come we hadn't heard about this one? You'd think this was the kind of information that Lola would have shared with us unless … I interrupted my own train of thought.

'Hey! Do you think Lola may have been involved in Josie's murder, and then Lily found out? She's big enough and probably strong enough to take those two on.' I looked at the other women.

'Maybe,' replied Leslie. 'I certainly could see Lola doing something like that, not planned, of course, but because she was just so mad at Josie.'

I had to agree. As someone famous once said, 'Hell hath no fury like a woman scorned.' Substitute 'angry at her husband for paying attention to another woman' for 'scorned' and we had ourselves a good motive for murder.

Still, the Julian Sweet angle needed further investigation, hence the trip to Manchester on the morrow.

We finally headed for bed. A form of détente, Becklaw-style, had been declared between the two older women and I was able to lay my head down relatively worry-free. At least the four of us would be safe from one another.

We actually did sleep through that night, unmolested by strange noises or another break-in. I had my coffee and toast, showered and dressed, and was ready to go when the boys showed up: Derek to drive us into Manchester and LJ to sit with Miss Lucinda.

With a wave and a caution to 'stay together and lock up if you leave', Miss Bea, Leslie, Derek, and I drove away. Miss Bea had rigged up a makeshift antenna with a wire clothes hanger and we were able to listen to some music – this time it was The Who and "Baba O'Riley" – on the way in to town. I even found myself humming along.

We had thought to call ahead and see if Officer Kingsley was available. She was, so we went directly to the Manchester Police Department. I gave our names at the front desk – the officer acted like he knew me – and we sat down to wait. Within just a few minutes, a smiling Officer Kingsley opened the door and beckoned for us to follow her.

Being somewhat familiar with the warren of hallways by this time, I realized that she was leading us to a conference room. That should have set off alarm bells for me, but I meekly trailed her and my companions trailed me.

When she opened the door, we saw that the room was nearly full of officers, each sitting with a stack of papers in front of them and the emblematic mug of bad coffee to hand. I halted in the doorway and nearly caused a pedestrian traffic jam.

'Come in and find a seat, you guys. You're just in time for a team briefing,' Officer Kingsley welcomed us in to the room. If I could have sunk through the floor, I would have. Talk about embarrassment!

Not to mention my wonderment at being included in an official briefing. This had all the aspects of a made-for-TV drama, where the local gal or guy helps to crack a case that has totally baffled the police. Not likely, Jo, I thought. Still, it was nice to get the invite.

The team briefing was on the dual murders. Motives were discussed and I recognized some of the things that we had shared with Officer K. All right – maybe we were more helpful than I had previously thought. I felt a tinge of self-pride well up but quickly squelched it; after all, karma was still hanging about and I didn't want to invite another casualty.

Per what we heard, the idea that Julian Sweet could be considered a suspect was plausible. Some officers were leaning toward the 'scorned woman' theory, and I was anxious to share with Officer Kingsley what we had discovered about Lola and her husband, Hap.

I tried to crane my neck without being obvious, reading over the shoulder of the officer nearest me. He had done nothing but doodle, the lined notepaper filled with fanciful swirls and happy faces. I wondered if Officer Kingsley was aware of this. I casually looked at another officer's notepad and saw much the same thing. Well. If that was the way things were handled in Manchester, it was no wonder two people could meet their end the way Josie and Lily had.

My confidence in their ability to solve these crimes went subterranean but fast. When the topic turned to 'What's for lunch' and 'Did you see the game last night', I was through. I motioned to Leslie, Miss Bea, and Derek to follow me and we stood to our feet.

'Officer K, thanks for allowing us to sit in on your ...' here I paused significantly and gave the doodling officers a Mrs Fiornelli fish-eye '... *meeting*, but we need to get back to Miss Lucinda. She, er ... hasn't been feeling well lately.'

We trooped out the conference room door and down the hall part-way before Derek, walking just behind me, asked, 'So? What do you think that was all about?'

I let him come abreast of me before replying. That hallway had some killer acoustics.

'Well, I think that was a "We have it all under control" invitation,' I said.

'I think so too,' Derek responded, reaching out to open the door at the end of the hallway. 'Which makes me think they don't. Have it under control, I mean,' he added for clarification.

The four of us stayed silent until we got out to the station wagon. I looked over my shoulder at Miss Bea, who sat next to Leslie in the back seat.

'Now what? Any ideas?'

Miss Bea shook her head slowly. 'No, Jo, I'm clean out of ideas on this. I tell you what: let's pick up some lunch for the six of us and head back to the trailer, maybe have a picnic. We might as well enjoy the rest of the day.'

I had to agree. For some reason the wind had gone out this entire affair and now I just wanted to enjoy what time was left of our visit to Silverton County.

We found a deli that advertised sandwiches to go, along with chips, whole dill pickles, and freshly-baked cookies. I tried to call LJ to see what he and Miss Lucinda would like, but got no answer. Instead, I left a message telling him to give me a call in the next few minutes, but said that if he didn't, Miss Bea would choose for him.

Not hearing from LJ, we settled on three foot-long sub sandwiches, six little bags of chips, four pickles (Leslie and I opted out), and a dozen cookies. We piled back into the station wagon and headed back to the KOA, picnic lunch in tow. We chattered about where we should go to eat. I suggested the tables just to the rear of the KOA. The McLaughlins had thoughtfully provided a Ramada-type shelter, making the area usable even on inclement days.

We pulled into the KOA, heading the station wagon toward the trailer where LJ was keeping an eagle eye on Miss Lucinda. I hoped he had survived; sometimes she could be a bit overbearing.

Carting one of the bags up the steps and onto the porch, I stopped short. The front door, locked when we had left a few hours before, now stood slightly open. That familiar prickle began its trip down my spine; something did not feel right. When I spotted the splintered wood of the door's frame, I froze.

Derek and Leslie, who had been chatting amiably about their respective homes, noticed my hesitation. I could see that Derek was going to call out so I waved my hand at him in a 'be quiet' gesture. Thank goodness he could read the Josephine Anderson version of sign language.

I tiptoed back off of the porch, holding my breath against tell-tale creaks of the weathered wood. Thank goodness I had learned to walk softly early in life; my prowess for sneaking out of the house at night was legendary among my many nieces and nephews.

Derek, Leslie, and Miss Bea were watching my progress with concern. I got within earshot of them and told them about the door's condition. I thought poor Miss Bea was going to faint. Instead, only her hair slipped a notch. She was a strong woman, emotionally speaking.

The four of us moved away from the trailer as slowly as we could; although I tell you, I was tempted to run like a bat out of … well, you get the idea. I wanted to get out of there as quickly as was humanly possible and get help.

Once we had made it past what I calculated was far enough away so as not to be heard by whoever was in there with Miss Lucinda and LJ, if indeed they were still there, I fished my cell out of my pocket and thumbed through the contacts until I reached Officer Kingsley's number. With shaking fingers I attempted to dial; it took three tries before I got it right.

When I heard her voicemail and that cheery voice admonishing to "Don't Worry, Be Happy", I almost wept in frustration. Now what? I had no idea who else to call and I was beside myself with worry. I could tell by the looks on the others' faces that they felt the same as I did.

'Now what?' I mouthed as quietly as possible, looking to Miss Bea for guidance.

She stood still a moment, thinking hard. At last, she said, 'Let's go up to the manager's office. We can tell them and use their phone.'

Head slap! Of course – why I hadn't I thought of that?

We hurried as fast as we could go, deli bags caught up in our arms as headed for the front of the KOA and help.

Chapter Twenty-eight

We four flew through the door of the office and paused, hesitating, not seeing either Percy or Oleta McLaughlin in the reception area. I walked over to the door that led to their private living quarters and knocked, head tilted toward the door to listen for any sound that might indicate whether they were in or not.

What I heard chilled me to the bone.

I motioned frantically for the others to join me and they did, a collective look of concern on their faces. I indicated that they should listen; one by one, they pressed their ears to the door and one by one they recoiled, a look of fear replacing the alarm.

What I had heard – and what they had now confirmed – was the sound of Miss Lucinda's voice as she begged for the McLaughlins to let her and LJ go. I tried once more to get Officer K on the line, and this time I had success. When I heard her hearty 'Officer Kingsley here,' I almost cried.

'This is Jo, Jo Anderson. We need you out here at the KOA pronto. The McLaughlins have Miss Lucinda and LJ ...' I was babbling and I knew it, but I couldn't stop myself.

'Slow down, Jo,' commanded Officer Kingsley, and her tone, authoritative and calm, arrested my thoughts enough to let them catch up to my mouth.

'We just got back to our trailer at the KOA and found the door kicked in. Miss Lucinda and LJ are up here at the office, and the McLaughlins are holding them captive.' I felt foolish saying this, but if it was true, I'd sound foolish all day long in order to ensure their safety.

Officer K did not question my statement but instead asked me for our location. I told her, and she suggested that we move away from the building as casually as possible, and she and backup would be on their way. We did as she had told me, but it was difficult to leave, knowing that Miss Lucinda and LJ could be in mortal danger.

We huddled together under the shade of the tallest aspen that stood just to the right of the driveway, eyes peering anxiously down the highway for any sign of Manchester's finest. I could have cried when I saw the first car, lights on but riding silently. It pulled to the side of the road a few yards from the KOA's entrance, a second car pulling up behind them.

Officer Kingsley exited the second car, talking into a radio and motioning us to join her. We waited for her to finish the transmission, a bit impatiently, I must admit, while the other officers walked over to join us. I recognized the two doodlers from the briefing, but they acted as though they had never seen me. Just as well, I thought; I might be tempted to give them a piece of my mind.

'OK.' Officer Kingsley looked around at those of us gathered, four of us anxious and the others with their game faces on and ready to rock and roll. 'This is what we'll do, per the Captain: Snow,' – doodler *numéro uno* – 'you and I will take the outside private entrance. Steadman, you and Shaw will take the private entrance located in the office. You other two,' – motioning to doodler *numéro dos* and a short, muscular officer whose badge read 'Peterson' – 'will cover the windows to the residence. We try to make contact first, then go in on my count if no answer. If that's the case, I'll count three and then we go in, got it?'

All officers nodded, and I found I'd been holding my breath. I moved closer to Miss Bea and put my arm around her, and Leslie took the other side. I could feel the older woman breathing rapidly, and I was afraid she'd hyperventilate. We needed to get her calmed down, at least as much as we could. I met Leslie's eyes over her head and we silently consented to gently move back against the tree we had been standing under to begin with. Derek followed, still carrying two of the bags containing our lunch.

Aha! My go-to remedy for any and all that ails you – sugar – was in the bag I carried. I had almost forgotten that we had purchased cookies of several different kinds to go with our sandwiches and chips. I opened the bag and pulled out a handful, passing them to the others indiscriminately. I had a chocolate chip, Leslie had oatmeal, and Derek and Miss Bea both had sugar iced ones with a thick frosting.

We munched the goodies as we watched the police move into place: two alongside the wall that was in our view; Officers Kingsley and Snow going around to the other side of the building; and the other two officers entering the office. I heard a faint crackle from the radio on one of the officer's shoulders and he spoke quietly into it, acknowledging Officer K's commands.

Looking back on that spring afternoon, I find that I have a few gaps that still haven't been filled. For instance, I don't recall the exact moment that the officers moved in, having gotten no answer from either the McLaughlins or their niece Lola, who had coerced them into joining her in the commission of the kidnappings and the two murders. I can't remember who came out first, the perpetrators or the victims, but I do know that suddenly I had my arms tightly around Miss Lucinda's ample waist, and that she and Miss Bea remained glued together for the rest of the time we spent in Manchester.

LJ, in spite of his naturally tentative veneer, seemed the least traumatized of us all. Leslie, on the other hand, could not let go of LJ's hand or arm, and before we left for Copper and home base, she was sporting an engagement ring. Apparently LJ had carried it around for quite a while. I realized that I had always been a bit curious about their relationship; for some reason, I had put them down as kissing cousins or best friends.

It turned out that they were both.

I suppose I should have suspected the McLaughlins and their niece all along, in hindsight, but there were other clues that had thrown me off – and threw the police off as well, Officer Kingsley admitted later. It seems that Lola's strategy was to be obvious about a possible motive – the 'scorned woman angle' – and hope that it would seem *too* obvious. It almost worked.

Lola's husband Hap was in shock over the entire episode, and the last I heard of him he was ensconced in the Silverton County Behavioral Center, being treated for clinical depression. Who could blame him? His wife had turned out to be as batty as her Aunt Oleta. Her Uncle Percy, poor thing, was roped into it all of it by reason of blackmail.

He had not paid taxes – state, local, or federal – for many years, and Lola knew about it. By some weird sense of reasoning, he figured it would be easier to get away with murder than to repay all that money.

People just baffle me at times, you know?

When the proverbial dust settled, we were amazed at

what we learned from Officer Kingsley over pizza and breadsticks on our last night at the KOA, which was now being run by Julian Sweet, who needed a more permanent job than the one at the casino.

'It keeps me away from gambling,' he confided to me, and I was glad for him. It also kept him away from Andy and Bert, who Julian had threatened to 'brain' if he ever spotted them within fifty yards of himself again. Not the brightest thing to declare publicly, but who could blame him?

Anyhoo, as they say back home in Piney Woods, Lola, carrying a deep grudge against Josie for breaking up her marriage – or, at least, that's what she truly thought, in spite of protestations from Hap – had overheard the gossip concerning Becklaw's Murder Mystery Tour and the fact that we would need locals to play some bit parts. Since Josie was never around, and Lola worked so many hours, she figured that if Josie had a part in the performance, she would know where she was and could confront her once and for all.

So, she passed along the suggestion to Skinny Joe via Lily, whom she knew from the library and who had told her about the available parts. In her mind, Josie was a perfect 'fit' for the 'lady of the night' part. Skinny Joe snapped up the proposal, eager to fulfill his end of the bargain, and had asked Josie to join the troupe and there you had it: the stage was set, so to speak, for a showdown.

Lily, we found out, had joined because of Andy, on whom she had a huge crush ever since their high school days. Any excuse to be near him thrilled her, and unfortunately, it also sealed her fate. She was also the only one who could directly connect Lola and Josie – so she had to be dealt with.

Lola, being the strong wench that she was, was able to

subdue Lily and well, you know the rest. I had seen her in action at the deli with the half ham, don't forget, so I had a clear idea of how she was able to … well, for the stomach's sake, I'll just leave it there.

Lola and Hap had arrived early for the barbecue supper and she watched the time carefully, calculating when the cast would be arriving. She was pretty close, too; she got to the parking lot just minutes before Josie pulled in.

The confrontation, which in Lola's jealousy-plagued mind was justified, did not go the way she thought it would. Josie had laughed at her, calling her 'fat' and 'ugly' and doing everything but say something about her mother. Lola snapped, picking up a large rock from the row that lined the parking lot and bashing Josie on the back of the head as she turned to walk away.

To make it look like a random killing, though, she had run to their truck parked just a few feet away and had pulled out one of Hap's old hunting pistols. Josie was already dead, or very close to it, when Lola had shot her.

The pistol had been recovered by Officer Snow and the ballistics tests had proven it was a match for the gun that fired the bullet recovered from Josie's body.

"The best laid plans of mice and men", I thought wryly. I think what troubled me the most was that Lola had almost gotten away with it and an innocent man, Julian Sweet, had almost taken the fall.

Back to Lily and her untimely demise: once she had realized that Josie was dead, and had figured pretty quickly who must be to blame, Lily had called into work and scheduled some personal time off. She had planned on leaving the area and going to her parents down in Denver, but never had the chance to leave town. The very next morning following Josie's murder, Lola had begun calling Lily, threatening that she'd get the same if she talked to anyone, 'anyone' being the Manchester Police Department.

This had the opposite effect on Lily, though; instead of scaring her into silence, it had made her angry at Lola. She dared her to come over and confront her, which was Mistake Number One.

The second blunder was when she unlocked the front door and let her in. The third error happened when she turned her back briefly on Lola, who had needed but a moment to hit Lily on the head with the large flashlight she had been carrying.

Officer Snow recovered this weapon as well, from the grocery store deli where Lola worked. She had brazenly taken it and brought it back, not even bothering to clean it off that well. She figured, with her twisted reasoning, that no one in the deli department would notice a little blood on the handle.

Apparently she was right. It had been sitting there in plain sight when we had stopped by that day.

The McLaughlins were dragged into the sordid affair when Lola found out that the troupe was staying at the KOA. She assumed that we might be interested in finding out who had done away with two of our cast members and had asked her aunt to spy on us. That was the noise on our walk the night before; Oleta McLaughlin, in her confession, told Officer Kingsley that Derek had given her a face full of dirt and pebbles.

I mentally gave Derek a high five.

Poor Percy McLaughlin was simply supposed to go over to the trailer and keep us occupied instead of us keeping our appointment with Officer Kingsley, which he knew about, after eavesdropping outside our open living room window while his wife was cleaning dirt out of her eyes. Unfortunately, when he had arrived, not only did he not have the master key he normally carried, but four of us had already left to keep the appointment.

Truly afraid of his niece Lola, he had kicked down the trailer's flimsy front door and had taken Miss Lucinda and LJ by complete surprise. It wasn't much of a chore to round them up and march them down to the KOA office. Anyone who might have been looking outside at that instant wouldn't have seen anything suspicious, just the kindly manager taking care of an issue for two of his happy campers.

Lola was already there, having arrived early in the morning and let herself into the McLaughlin's private residence with a key she'd had made on the sly. That threw her aunt off guard, and when Percy had turned up with his two prisoners, Oleta had nearly had a nervous breakdown. Things had gotten completely out of hand, she had complained to Officer Kingsley, but what were she and her husband to do? They were victims as well.

Thank goodness the District Attorney did not see things her way, I thought.

Percy and Oleta McLaughlin were formally charged and indicted on second degree kidnapping since there was no intent to harm either Miss Lucinda or LJ. They were also facing charges of 'aiding and abetting' for helping Lola in her dirty scheme. They were looking at plenty of time to think about what they had done, we were assured.

As for Lola, she was definitely looking at some serious time behind bars. The evidence showed a cold calculation in the planning and commission of the two deaths, and she was charged and indicted on two counts of first degree murder as well as the second degree kidnapping charges, although I personally do not agree with that. I truly believed that she would have hurt or even killed Miss Lucinda and LJ, as well as her own flesh and blood. That woman was just plain nuts.

Speaking of crazy women naturally brought my thoughts back to Crazy Great-Aunt Opal and Piney Woods, Louisiana. I had missed her – and my home – more than I cared to admit. I wasn't ready to throw in the proverbial towel, though; I had contracted with Miss Bea and Becklaw's Murder Mystery Tour for six months, and six months it would be.

Chapter Twenty-nine

With our stay in Manchester over at last, we had packed up and set off for Copper early in the morning. This time, we traveled as a group of six; Miss Bea had asked Miss Lucinda to come back with us and to consider making Copper her home.

I was delighted. With Leslie and LJ mooning over one another and Derek sinking back into his role of Reticent Man, I needed some lively conversation to stimulate my mind. Miss Lucinda certainly fit the bill.

The trip back to Copper flew by. The sisters-in-law kept me entertained with stories of their early meeting, of Desmond and Beatrice's courtship and subsequent marriage, and of the many trips around the United States and the world they had taken. I was amazed at just how different the Becklaw family was from my own. The Anderson clan would have never even considered a trip to another state, much less one that required obtaining a passport and crossing deep bodies of water.

Shortly after the sun had sunk into its western bed, drawing cloudy curtains of purples and oranges and pinks around it for the night, we reached the turn-off for the town of Copper and Miss Bea's house. I was tired, my backside was numb, and my mind was still full of the events of the previous few days. All I wanted was a hot shower and a good night's sleep in my own bed. I briefly wondered where Miss Lucinda would be sleeping, then figured that she would bunk in with Miss Bea; those two had really become inseparable.

The driveway to the house had never looked so sweet to me. I started grinning at the beginning of the rough, bumpy trail and didn't quit until my head hit the pillow that night. I was sure glad to be back and in one piece.

None of us were hungry enough to make a proper meal, and the refrigerator had been cleared out before our jaunt up to Manchester. I rummaged around and found a frozen loaf of bread and a jar of peanut butter. Peanut butter on toast would have to do for dinner. I'd need to restock before too long or I'd starve to death.

With my stomach finally full and with a glass of cool well water in hand, I went up the creaking stairs to my room. Leslie had already retired for the night, tired from all that lovey-dovey handholding, I thought wryly. I tiptoed past her door on my way to the bathroom, not wanting to wake her. She would need her rest to get ready for another day of billing and cooing.

I made my toilette and returned to my room, happy to be home, or at least to be in Miss Bea's comfortable house. I walked across the room, careful to look at my feet as I stepped on the wooden floor, not wanting to make the acquaintance of another mouse. I unlatched and pushed open the window, leaning out into the cool, crisp Colorado night.

My thoughts turned toward Piney Woods, and the wistfulness I had managed to push down during the day welled back up in full force. I was, to put it succinctly, well and truly homesick.

I thought about my seven brothers, about how they had alternately made my childhood happy, terrifying, mysterious, and delightful in turns. I let my mind wander through thoughts of their many offspring, their spouses and their houses, and I had to smile. I had a wonderful family.

I thought about Crazy Great-Aunt Opal and our many visits together at her 'luxury apartment', of the many hands of gin rummy we had played and the jokes we had told one another ... and played on the other residents. I could hardly wait to see her again and tell her about Lola; that was one gal who could rival my Great-Aunt for sheer kookiness, I reflected.

And finally, I thought about Mama: about her carefully coiffed hair and always neat clothes; of her cool hands on my forehead when I was sick; and her sweet voice reading a myriad of bedtime stories to me when I was a child. I felt my throat tighten and my eyes fill with tears, and I leaned my head onto my folded arms and let myself 'weep a little weep', as my mother would say.

Wiping my eyes, I made up my mind: I would ask Miss Bea in the morning if I could be released from the troupe. With that settled, I closed the window, got into bed, and promptly fell asleep.

The morning light moved across my face and awakened me. I stretched, holding my arms up high in the air while I reached to the end of the bed with my bare toes ... and froze. Something tiny and furry was moving down there.

I leapt out of bed faster than I had ever had before. Leslie told me later that I sounded as though a strange language was coming from my mouth with nothing making sense. I can only remember clutching at her arms and pointing frantically at my bed.

Derek, once again, was my savior. He flipped back the covers and retrieved the frightened little mouse that had burrowed further down toward the end of the mattress, trying to get away from the crazy girl and her big feet. I huddled closer to Leslie as Derek walked past with the tiny creature in his cupped palms. LJ, who had joined the crowd gathered in my room, followed Derek down the stairs and held open the front door for him, allowing the frightened mouse to make good his escape.

Miss Bea and Miss Lucinda, awakened by all the commotion, stood side by side in the front room, nightgowns billowing around their legs, which were surprisingly spindly considering the other proportions of their bodies.

I wasn't sure whose hair defied gravity the most: Miss Bea's or Miss Lucinda's. It was an amazing sight, the tufts of frizzy grey and hanks of lavender hanging this way and that. I managed to keep my face straight though; these two women had been like fairy godmothers to me.

I resorted to my typical method of handling any crisis involving a creature and marched directly into the kitchen for a round of enthusiastic cooking. This morning's episode required something hearty and satisfying, so I decided to whip up my mother's famous Piney Woods Pecan Pancakes. Bare cupboards yawned back at me in the early morning light; time for that trip into town.

With a less than enthusiastic Derek at the wheel of Miss Bea's wagon (he'd made movements back toward his bed but I nixed that), we set off for Copper in hopes of finding at least one store open. I was a woman on a mission and after all I'd been through, securing the ingredients for a real Louisiana breakfast seemed like small potatoes, if you catch my drift.

At last, we were gathered at the breakfast table, stacks of the steaming cakes on each plate, thick with real butter and maple syrup, a heaping platter of crispy bacon standing within reach of the six of us.

We ate in comparative silence for a while, making comments on the day's plans and the food; no one, I noticed, even mentioned Mouse Incident Part *Deux*. Maybe they just assumed that I attracted critters the way some folks attracted mosquitoes.

My talk with Miss Bea went much easier than I thought it would. We both cried a bit and laughed a lot, and hugged each other like the mother and daughter we had become. I thanked her over and over again for my foray into the world of character acting – neither of us mentioned that we actually only performed the Murder Mystery Tour once – and it was confirmed that I would depart in two days' time.

I spent the rest of my time in Copper relaxing with my friends, exchanging email addresses and cellphone numbers. Leslie assured me that I would be invited to the wedding, and LJ, to my surprise, unlatched from his intended and gave me a hug farewell when it was time for me to board the train back to Piney Woods. Derek gave me a salute, then turned back to help Miss Bea and Miss Lucinda back across the station platform and down the stairs. He was staying on indefinitely, he had confided; this was home to him in a way that no other place had ever been. I fervently wished him all the best. He'd need it, dealing with the Becklaw gals day after day.

Goodbyes over and done with, I settled back into my seat, determined to rest on the eight-hour trip. I was not going to make eye contact with anyone this time, I promised myself, especially if they had lavender hair.

Epilogue

The 06:36 train pulled into the Piney Woods station some fifteen minutes late, which to the locals meant 'right on time'. I could see a contingent of Andersons standing off to one side of the platform, talking, laughing at something that had been said, and their hands swiping fondly across shoulders, the mass of children running around screaming and having a raucously good time.

My family. They weren't perfect, but they were *mine*.

The cars jerked to a full stop and I stood up, ready to disembark. I was stiff from sitting in one place for so long; in fact, I'd slept most of the way. I retrieved my cases, joined the queue in the aisle, and stepped off the train … straight into the open arms of my mother. Her eyes were bright and she looked as if she would cry at any moment.

Time to head that one off at the pass, I thought. I gave her a tight squeeze.

'Hey, Mama! I was just thinking: have you ever thought about training my useless brothers to do something worthwhile, like maybe a circus act?'

She dropped her arms, giving me that familiar indignant look. I smiled. I was home.

Also by Dane McCaslin
Murder at the Miramar

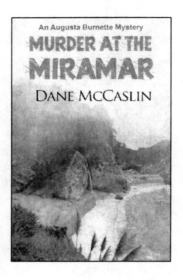

For more information about **Dane McCaslin**
and other **Accent Press** titles
please visit

www.accentpress.co.uk

CPSIA information can be obtained at www.ICGtesting.com
Printed in the USA
LVOW11s1713070314

376490LV00001B/16/P